PRAISE FOR A. J. BANNER

#1 Amazon, *USA Today*, and *Publishers Weekly* bestseller

"A. J. Banner sets up her mystery perfectly."

—*National Post*

"Banner's ability to maintain tension while teasing out the truth . . . keep[s] readers engaged."

—*Publishers Weekly*

"A. J. Banner is a truly gifted storyteller!"
—Wendy Walker, *USA Today* bestselling author of *All Is Not Forgotten*

THE
POISON
GARDEN

OTHER BOOKS BY
A. J. BANNER

The Good Neighbor
The Twilight Wife
After Nightfall

THE
POISON
GARDEN

A.J. BANNER

LAKE UNION
PUBLISHING

Text copyright © 2019 by Anjali Writes LLC
All rights reserved.

Published by Lake Union Publishing, Seattle

www.apub.com

Amazon, the Amazon logo, and Lake Union Publishing are trademarks of Amazon.com, Inc., or its affiliates.

ISBN-13: 9781542004237 (hardcover)
ISBN-10: 1542004233 (hardcover)
ISBN-13: 9781542042888 (paperback)
ISBN-10: 1542042887 (paperback)

Cover design by Rex Bonomelli

Printed in the United States of America

First edition

THE
POISON
GARDEN

PROLOGUE

I am running through the woods in the waning moonlight, splatters of blood on my hands, the wind whipping in from the sea. Tall firs bend and sway, branches crackling, breaking in the gale. I am lost but must keep moving. I once knew these trails, could find my way with my eyes closed, but that was long ago. The forest has twisted and grown, the shadows no longer familiar. My feet are dragging, pain squeezing my ribs, a throbbing in my skull.

The path splits here, the left track climbing upslope, the right plunging into darkness. I must choose a direction—it's life or death. The sum of my choices has brought me here. Every decision I've made, every suspicion I've nurtured or ignored, has led me into danger.

I choose the path to the left, uphill—I don't remember this route. Thorns snag my jeans, slowing me down. I see it now, a faint beacon of light blinking in a distant window.

I follow the glow, but it fades from view, then reappears brighter. The oxygen clots in my lungs, each breath an effort. Thudding footfalls approach behind me, catching up, then the trail bursts open, dumping me into the garden. I've come full circle, back home again.

Ahead of me, the Victorian rises against the inky sky. I'm so close, almost there, stumbling past sunflowers bowing in a gust of air, the tangled privet hedge, the reflecting garden pond. At the edges of my vision, I see the lights in the backyard cottage, the bulbs ablaze, their radiance reflected in the many sashed windows.

No stopping now, but all the strength is draining from my limbs. Fragmented scenes flit through my mind—fog swirling beneath an antique streetlamp, deadly nightshade berries gleaming in the rain, the Juliet flower erupting into poisonous bloom.

The footfalls thump right behind me. The breathing, the swiping of boots through the grass. Someone beyond the cottage is calling my name. "Elise! Elise, stop!"

I'm too slow—it's too late. I am falling into the grass. The garden fades at its edges, disappearing, all hope dissolving into the night.

CHAPTER ONE

Three days earlier

On the ferry ride home, I was not yet planning to kill anyone. I was still full of hope, eager to land on Chinook Island, although the rocking boat made me queasy, pitching and rolling on the churning waters of Rosario Strait. I tried to focus on a seagull riding an updraft alongside my window, its feathers ruffling in the breeze. *Our first wedding anniversary is tomorrow,* I thought to the bird. *What do you think of that?*

The seagull called out sharply, seeming to cry, *Congrats!* It was a male Thayer's gull, I guessed, gray and white with a spot of orange on its bill. Kieran would know for sure. He'd turned me on to bird-watching, bought me my first pair of binoculars.

I would bring them on our next sailing adventure, a weekend tour of the islands. We could leave earlier than planned, as I'd cut short my stay in Seattle by one day to surprise him.

I'd met with my financial adviser, as I'd promised I would. What had been mine was now also Kieran's. I'd also shopped for lavish anniversary gifts, and I'd stopped by the herbal fair to pick up supplies for my shop, all the while daydreaming, playing back the night before I'd left, when a September storm had pummeled the island, and Kieran and I had lain in the warmth of our bed, limbs entwined. I couldn't wait to get home.

I kept scrolling through pictures of him on my phone. Rugged features, startling blue eyes, and windswept russet hair. He'd gained a little weight around the middle, which only made him more attractive to me, more human. There he was, sailing his yacht in a summer breeze, helping me blow out thirty-six candles on my birthday cake, singing to me in a video in that smooth baritone. A little off-key, but charming. He loved to kiss the palm of my hand, then all the way up my arm, and the morning I'd left for the city, he'd slipped a heart-shaped greeting card into my purse: *Here's to a lifetime together.*

The ferry slowed as we approached the island, Chinook Harbor emerging from the mist, the downtown strip of shops nestled against a hilly, forested background. In the protected bay, a variety of boats bobbed along a grid of floating docks. Kieran's yacht, the *Knot on Call*, was tied to the outermost slip, undulating gently on the waves. Fog shimmered in the air, lending the scene a mystical aura.

All along the waterfront, quaint boutiques huddled together in the autumn chill. From Chinook Pizza in its redbrick building to the shops in historic Victorians, the town had always felt like home. I loved the hidden alleys leading to backstreet cafés and art galleries, prime attractions for tourists.

I could always identify them, the tourists on the boat. Today, the first escapees were arriving from the city for a long weekend away. They looked ragged and world-weary. As the ferry neared the dock, they gathered at the salt-speckled windows, snapping photos on their phones.

Mostly for their benefit, the captain announced over the loudspeaker: "We are now arriving at Chinook Island. All passengers must disembark the vessel." This was the end of the line for the rusty ferry, before it would power up again and limp back to Anacortes, the launch point on the mainland to the San Juan Islands.

I descended the metal stairs to the car deck and got into my Honda just as the boat thudded against the dock. It took a minute for the ferry workers to secure the lines and lower the ramp over the water. When a woman in a yellow uniform summoned us forward, I started the car and followed the other vehicles off the boat.

As I drove past my favorite haunts on Waterfront Road—the Egret Bookstore, Orca Gifts, the Salmon Café—I could feel the languid island atmosphere seeping into me. In hanging baskets, petunias and geraniums still bloomed in a rainbow of vibrant colors.

The Sweet Dreams bakery rolled by, and I smiled at the memory of Kieran and me at the little window table, "our" table, where we'd first met nearly three years ago, just before my mother's initial diagnosis. We'd dated on and off after that, when I'd returned to visit her—it hadn't seemed weird to go out with her doctor. But when her condition worsened, the tumors spreading fast, I broke things off with him. He'd gotten way too serious, and I was so worried about my mother.

Then she suddenly passed away—from a stroke unrelated to her cancer—and I returned to the island, distraught. Kieran offered his shoulder, helped me arrange her memorial service, and the rest was history. I adored everything about him now, from his casual whistling to the silly faces he made at babies.

He hadn't yet returned my texts this morning, but he was probably busy with appointments. This time of year, patients came down with more coughs and colds. I imagined him flitting in and out of exam rooms, his white coat flapping behind him.

As though on cue, a text pinged on my phone, but not from him. It was from my ex-husband, Brandon. I'm in town for a project. Meet up for coffee? *Not a chance*, I thought with a prick of irritation. *Prick* being the operative word to describe him. He'd allowed me to endure painful fertility treatments for weeks, when the problem had been his all along. The death knell for our four-year marriage: he'd kept his low sperm count hidden from me until I'd found the medical report in his coat pocket. Too bad he still lived in Seattle, still built homes on the island. He seemed destined to keep turning up.

To purge him from my mind, I pulled over and hit speed dial for Kieran's cell phone. I knew I was bothering him, but I needed to hear his voice. He answered immediately. "Hey, beautiful. I miss you."

"Hey, Dr. Lund," I said, relief spreading through me.

"So the meeting with the adviser went well?"

"Yes, and—"

"Ready to trade in the Honda for an upgrade?"

"I'll drive this old thing until it dies."

"That's my wife." His voice dropped to a purr. "I can't wait to hold you."

I grinned, riding a flush of pleasure. "I love you," I said. Barely a mile from the clinic, it was all I could do not to drive there and announce my early return.

"I love you more."

I hung up, my heart buoyant as I drove the last two miles to Lost Bluff Lane. Our elegant blue Victorian, my childhood home, was the second of only three widely spaced houses on a quiet cul-de-sac. The bungalow on the corner was empty, for sale, and our neighbor, Chantal Gittner, lived at the end of the lane. All three houses backed onto a hundred acres of forest and trails leading to a windswept beach.

My herb shop sat in the woods behind our house, the little blue cottage's myriad sashed windows reflecting the lush gardens. I'd kept the Clary Sage open to honor my mother, but I'd diversified, carrying more gift items to complement her medicinal teas, salves, and tinctures. I'd admired her intuitive approach to healing, which did not come naturally to me. As a pharmacist, I couldn't help my scientific leaning. I'd studied chemistry, physics, and mathematics—pharmacists were much more than pill counters. We understood the interactions among medications and the structures of chemical bonds. We filled hundreds of scrips per day. But the pressures of the job had worn me down, and when my mother died, I returned to a slower life on the island. I relished the challenges of gardening and shopkeeping, but I had not yet mastered her expertise at creating effective botanical remedies.

I parked next to the main house, and as I hoisted my suitcase from the trunk of my car, I could hear the deep drumbeat of distant salsa music. Curious. Normally I couldn't hear any noise from Chantal's house, a few acres through the trees. *She must be throwing a wild party,* I thought. But in the middle of the day?

Maybe kids were camping in the woods, blaring music from a boom box. I shielded my eyes and gazed toward the forest. Nothing but trees, shadows, and the distant glimmer of the ocean.

As I rolled my luggage through the front garden and up to the porch, the music grew louder. It was coming from inside our house. My heartbeat quickened. Somebody was here, but it couldn't be Kieran. There was no other car in the driveway.

Maybe someone had broken in—unlikely in our remote location, but one never knew. The intruder might've rowed ashore in a canoe, but again, not likely given the hostile currents on this side of the island.

I unlocked the front door and it swung open silently. "Hello?" I called out cautiously, peering inside. The din of the music swallowed my voice. I rolled my suitcase into the foyer and closed the door after me. A sandalwood scent wafted through the air. The hallway stretched back to the kitchen, the dining room on my right, the living room on my left. Nothing appeared to be amiss, but the music pounded in my brain, Spanish lyrics blaring from the stereo in the living room. Kieran's favorite album. Was he here? Then where was his car?

I left my suitcase by the front door, spotted his black loafers on the floor—next to a smaller pair of women's ballet flats. The shoes were not mine, and neither was the pink canvas tote bag with rope handles sitting on the foyer table next to Kieran's wallet and phone and a large pile of mail.

Had he parked around the corner for some unfathomable reason, or had he arrived home some other way? Who was with him? A sales rep, maybe, here for a business meeting. But why meet at home? It didn't make sense.

I took off my shoes. "Hello?" I called out again. "Kieran?"

No answer. I peeked into the living room. Nobody was there. The music kept pounding from the stereo. The family photos watched me from the mantel—Kieran and I at the wedding with our closest friends, my mother on her various trips to gardens around the world. She seemed to cringe at the blaring music. I considered turning down the volume, but then Kieran would know I was home. I preferred to remain incognito as I backed up into the hall.

Muffled voices drifted down the stairs, threading in and out of spaces in the song. Kieran and his companion were on the second floor. I broke out in a sweat, my breathing shallow.

I climbed the stairs, instinctively avoiding the creaky step, the one I'd learned to skip when I'd sneaked out at night as a teenager. Not that anyone could hear through the racket. When I reached the top of the stairs, the smell of sandalwood grew stronger. The voices were louder, too—I heard a woman's tinkling laughter, and then a familiar guffaw. They were most likely in the master bedroom, which overlooked the back garden, giving no view of the driveway.

Kieran was supposed to be at work. But those were his shoes downstairs. His wallet, his phone. My insides twisted, the hairs rising on my skin.

The song playing below ended, and in the moments before the next one began, I heard a loud groan. The next song started, a slower, melancholy beat, a woman's voice crooning in Portuguese.

I floated outside myself as I approached the master bedroom. I became aware of every flaw in the grain of the wood floor, worn sections of paint on the hallway walls. The bedroom door stood slightly ajar. I stayed out of sight, the music muted at this distance. The bed squeaked as someone got up, footsteps heading somewhere.

". . . take a piss," Kieran said.

"Hurry up," a woman said. "We don't have all day." The voice sounded familiar.

"I could cancel the rest of my appointments," Kieran called out. "We could fuck all afternoon."

I flinched at the word, an assault on my eardrums. I froze, my hands curling into fists.

"We'll have plenty of time," she replied. I heard the flick of something, and then the acrid odor of cigarette smoke wafted through the air. She'd lit a cigarette in my house, in my bed.

"Why not this afternoon?" Kieran said from the bathroom. "We're here now."

The woman laughed. "We've got the rest of our lives."

The ballad crooned on downstairs, while I stood motionless. *The rest of their lives,* which I imagined would be barely a minute before I murdered them both.

I heard a stream of urine hit the toilet bowl, then the flush, water running in the bathroom sink.

"Hey, you can't smoke in here," Kieran said, coming back into the bedroom. I recognized the serrated edge of irritation in his voice, so rare that it stood out.

"Oh, come on," she said. Scuffling, another toxic tendril of smoke creeping into my nose.

"Open the damn window," Kieran said. "Don't be an idiot. Elise has a keen sense of smell."

"Like a dog," the woman said. The window slid open.

"More like a cat. A cute, sleek cat."

"Don't talk about her that way," the woman said, a pout in her voice. "I don't want to do this."

"Do what? Enjoy yourself?" The squeaking of the mattress again, Kieran getting in beside her, maybe.

Sweat had broken out on my forehead, in my armpits, my heartbeat fast. Still, I didn't move.

"I want it to be done," she said, her voice slightly muffled.

"You have to learn to play the long game."

"Yeah, well, I wish she could just be gone already."

"Patience. Chill out."

You'll be the ones gone, I thought. *Both of you, out of my house.*

Then the rhythm began, the creaking of the box springs, that timeless, iconic, horrifying sound, and downstairs, the next song banging to life.

CHAPTER TWO

Time slowed. The world stopped turning. Every particle of dust hung suspended in the air. Then I flung open the bedroom door so hard, the knob slammed against the wall. I strode in and stood at the foot of the bed, shaking all over. The stench of smoke assaulted my nose.

Kieran rolled off the woman and she sat up, gasping, her red mouth in an O of surprise. I caught a glimpse of dark nipples as she clutched the comforter to her chest. Sculpted face, long red hair. Gray eyes, fake lashes black and thick. She was so thin, she looked breakable. And young. Her name hovered on the tip of my tongue—Diane something. Jasper. Diane Jasper. Kieran had hired her to stage his farmhouse, the home he was selling, now that he had moved in with me. I had met her only once, had thought her friendly.

Kieran leaped to his feet naked, shouting, "Elise, what are you doing here?" He was not a tall man, but his broad shoulders gave him an imposing presence. Those rough features, that unkempt hair, those penetrating eyes. He made me catch my breath, even now when I hated him.

"I live here," I answered coldly.

"I'm leaving," Diane said, scrambling out of bed, reaching for a pair of jeans that lay on the floor like deflated legs. She grabbed for a shiny tank top, breasts jiggling.

Kieran, not bothering to get dressed, tried to reach for me. I stepped back and held out my hand to keep him away. I took in the clothing tossed about, the massage oil on the nightstand. The complete disarray, the trespass. I was trembling. I dashed through the bedroom into the bathroom and heaved into the toilet. I could hear Kieran and Diane scrabbling around as I rinsed my mouth at the sink, splashed cold water on my face.

In the mirror my cheeks were flushed, my dark eyes glassy. A strange, wild-haired woman gazed back at me. The overhead light bulb flickered—a lacy black bra hung over the towel rack. I averted my gaze, drew another deep breath, thought to myself, *Get a grip.*

When I returned to the bedroom, Diane had pulled on a sweater, her hair caught in the collar. Kieran paced in his briefs. He might've been speaking, trying to explain, but his words blurred in my ears.

Diane slipped out the door and down the stairs in a whoosh of sandalwood. Without her lacy bra. I could have gone after her, but my legs wouldn't move. My brain kept trying to erase what was happening. The music stopped; the front door slammed.

Kieran came up to me and rested his hands on my shoulders. "What are you doing here? You weren't supposed to be home."

You're not supposed to fuck someone else, no matter where I am, I thought. My shoulders stiffened against his touch. What was that smell coming off him? Musk, his man smell, and something else—some*one* else.

"Where is your suitcase?" he said.

"Downstairs," I said, shrugging away from him. What did it matter where anything was?

"When did you get back? You were supposed to come home tomorrow."

"I took the morning ferry." I was surprised at how detached I felt. I was far away, flying across the sea with the Thayer's gull, catching an updraft into oblivion. Our marriage was over. So soon after it had begun.

"Why today?" he said, pacing, running his fingers through his hair.

"I wanted to surprise you. But you don't get to ask the questions."

He pressed the heel of his hand to his forehead, as if to hold in his brain. "How long were you standing in the hall?"

"Long enough. But that was a question. Here's one for you: What the hell is going on? Wait, don't answer that. I think it was obvious."

"There's nothing between Diane and me—it was an impulsive thing, a mistake. She came on to me." He tried to reach for my hand, but I slapped him away.

"I heard what she said. She wanted me to just be gone." I paced, crossing my arms over my middle, where I felt a biting pain.

He shook his head, his face pale, and rubbed at his chin. "She's the jealous type. I don't feel anything for her."

But he had brought her here, into our bed. "That's even worse. You married me, but you can still . . . do that. With someone you don't even care about?"

"That's not what I mean—it was just . . ."

"What? Sex?"

"Yeah, I guess so."

"Patience," I spat at him. "That's what you said—'patience.'"

He squinted at me, as if I'd just shone a bright light in his face. "I was trying to pacify her."

"And what's the 'long game,' Kieran? What do you want from me?" At the bed, I pulled off my pillowcase, threw it on the floor. It was contaminated now. I would wash the whole pillow, the mattress, the entire room.

"It was just talk. I don't remember what I said. She's . . . clingy. I was putting her off."

"So you led her on, the way you've been leading me on?"

"No! You're twisting things around. I love you." He closed his eyes, pressed his hands to his temples, then reached out for me again. But I slipped around to the other side of the bed, whipped off his pillowcase, too, and threw it on the floor.

"Spare me," I said. "How long have you been doing this? How many nights in this room?"

"Just today." He picked up the pillowcase and dropped it on the bed. He hated anything left on the floor. But he hadn't seemed bothered by Diane's clothing strewn everywhere. His, too.

I grabbed the bottle of massage oil, threw it in the garbage can. A tiny voice in my head said, *Be good to the earth. Recycle the container.* I wished to recycle Kieran and Diane as well. Or throw them into a trash compactor.

"I don't know what came over me," he said, blinking.

"What, she ambushed you? You were hypnotized?" I yanked off the bedcover. The pillowcase fell onto the floor again.

"She wouldn't leave me alone." He looked genuinely pained, his face contorted. He stepped back, and this time he did not pick up anything off the floor.

"And you succumbed to her feminine wiles? What century are you living in?" I started pulling off the mattress protector, glad it was waterproof.

"But that's the way it happened," he said. "Look, Elise, stop. Do you have to do this now? You're losing control of yourself."

"Like you lost control of your dick?" I shouted.

He ran his fingers through his hair again, but they got stuck in the tangles. "You're yelling."

What had I become? What had he made me into? I could've demanded to know how he could say he loved me on the phone, then five minutes later sleep with Diane. Or maybe at the same time. I could've asked where they had done it, only here or in his farmhouse, too? Had he cheated before, on his ex-wife? All the declarations of love, the plans we'd made—had they all been lies?

The answers didn't matter. I couldn't dwell on what could not be changed. It was done. He had done it.

"Elise?" he was saying, shaking my shoulders.

I didn't reply, realized I'd been standing by the window, swaying, the bedclothes in piles on the floor. "Let go of me. Don't touch me."

"You're in shock. Sit down. We'll talk. We can work this out."

His voice receded, the buzzing of an insect in my ear. *We will never talk*, I thought, *not now. Not ever.*

"Go," I said. "Get out of here."

He rested his hands on his hips. "You don't mean that. I can't just go. My car is at the clinic. Diane drove me here."

"I don't care. Go." My voice was soft, even. The window was open a little, the smell of smoke gone, replaced by the damp scents of moss and leaves.

"We have to talk—we have to work this out. Right now you're angry. You have a right to be angry."

"Get out of my house," I said, stepping over the pile of sheets.

"I'll go, okay, but let's talk. It just happened, okay? Like I said. It's not serious."

I strode past him and down the stairs. I could hear his footsteps behind me, muted thumps as he was barefoot. He kept nattering on, apologizing, saying he loved me. Blah, blah. I walked back through the hall into the kitchen. He'd left dirty dishes in the sink.

My hand shaking, I pulled out a large knife from the wooden block on the countertop. I looked at the blade, gleaming beneath the ceiling bulb, and I floated outside myself again.

When I turned around, he was standing in the open doorway, his eyes wide. I brandished the knife. "Get out."

"What are you doing? Put that down."

"What part of 'get out' do you not understand?"

He raised his hands, as if I were pointing a gun at him. "Okay, I'll go. I'm going."

"Good." I had no idea what I was doing. I needed to scare him. I needed him to leave. I needed a weapon against my pain. I advanced toward him.

He backed down the hall, his face white with shock. "Put the knife down. I'm leaving. I just need to get dressed, okay?"

"I don't care what you need."

He grabbed a coat from the front closet. "Here. I'm going, okay? I need to put on my shoes."

"Hurry up." I stepped toward him, my hand shaking. I knew I had lost my mind, but I couldn't help myself.

He shoved his feet into his loafers, grabbed his phone and wallet off the table. Diane's ballet flats and tote bag were gone.

"You don't want to hurt anyone," Kieran said, opening the front door. "You don't want to hurt yourself."

"You should've thought of that before you broke our vows." I was screaming inside, but my voice came out eerily quiet.

"What about my clothes?" He was out the door in his briefs and coat and shoes. The cold, damp air wafted inside. "I have patients. I need to go to work."

"So go to work. You'll find something to wear, maybe a hospital gown? Or one of those paper drapes patients wear in the exam room."

"Look, I can't just . . . I'll have to come back later. When you're calm."

"I am calm."

"We'll work this out. I'll call you."

"Don't patronize me," I said.

"I need my keys. I left them here somewhere."

"You've got spares. You'll survive." But I wasn't sure I would. My head was spinning. I held up the knife, and he stumbled down the walk toward the driveway. I watched him go, my heart pounding. He disappeared behind the trees, and I dropped the knife—it clattered to the floor. The thing was blunt anyway. Spots danced in front of my eyes. My legs weakened. I couldn't catch my breath. The edges of my vision darkened. I stumbled into the living room toward the couch, and the carpet rushed up to meet me, the lights winking into blackness.

CHAPTER THREE

"Elise, Elise, wake up." A familiar, feathery voice brushed at my ears. I looked up into the broad, elegant features of our neighbor, Chantal Gittner. Her crystal earrings glinted in the light, her emerald eyes wide and worried.

I lay on the carpet in the living room, a throw pillow under my head. She leaned over me, a swath of coffee-colored hair falling over her face as she tucked another pillow beneath my knees. I caught a whiff of her subtle floral perfume.

"What happened?" I said, blinking, looking around. I strained to focus on the sparse living-room furniture, the brick fireplace. The sunlight slanting in through the windows. My mother gazed at me from her photos on the walls—in each one she posed in a different country holding a rare, exotic plant. Even she looked worried. I avoided looking at the wedding photos.

Chantal flipped her hair behind her shoulder and frowned at me, her bottom lip protruding slightly. "What's going on? I was out for a run, and I saw Kieran on his phone in just a coat, no pants!"

"It's the new fashion," I said, sitting up.

"He got into an old Prius." She sat back on her heels. Her T-shirt, reading TECH NINJA, looked a size too small, accentuating her lean, sinewy muscles. The woman didn't have an ounce of fat on her bones.

"Good riddance," I said.

Her carefully plucked eyebrows rose like the arcing wings of a seagull. "Did you two have an argument? I ran up here and your door was wide open. Did he hurt you? You were out cold."

I rubbed my head—no blood. That was good. "No, I'm okay. How long was I unconscious?"

"A minute or two? I don't know." Chantal's gaze slid to the knife on the floor. Her mouth dropped open. "Did he try to use that on you?"

"What? No. I was the one holding the knife."

She looked at me askance. "You were?"

I rubbed my forehead, took a deep breath. "I only wanted to scare him. I wasn't going to stab him or anything." The truth was, I didn't know what I would've done if Kieran had refused to leave.

"Maybe I should call 9-1-1." She pulled a cell phone from her pocket. "I forgot, no signal here. When are you going to get the landline fixed?"

"The connections are rusted in the box outside," I said faintly. "They need to be replaced."

"What if you ever need to call someone?" She waved her cell phone in the air, this way and that, then tucked it into the back pocket of her jogging pants. "I'm not getting a signal."

"We walk down the driveway to make calls," I said. "But I don't need to call anyone. I'm fine. I must've just fainted." I got up and staggered onto the couch. "It was supposed to be a happy day, but . . ."

"Must've been a bad fight for you to threaten him with a knife."

"You don't know the half of it," I said.

"I'll get you a glass of water, okay? You relax."

"You don't have to get into the middle of this."

"I'm your friend. It's where I need to be, in the middle of this. Rest, okay? Can I get you anything else?"

"Just the water, thanks. Hey, I should be asking you. You're the guest here."

"I know where the kitchen is. Take it easy."

"Thank you, Chantal. You're a lifesaver." I leaned back against the couch cushion. My limbs felt like liquid, fatigue pushing on my chest. As I listened to the faucet running in the kitchen, I looked at my favorite wedding picture, displayed on the mantel. The photographer had captured a perfect moment, right after Kieran and I had recited the vows we had written ourselves. The pale September sun reflected off his hair. My cream-colored lace gown looked almost golden. Kieran had worn a black patterned vest beneath a silvery tuxedo jacket. He had just slid the wedding band, with its intricate carving of a seafaring knot, onto my finger. He was still holding my hand, and we gazed at each other in adoration, my face upturned to his.

I tried to detect a trace of deception in his expression, in the downward tilt of his chin. In the way he held my hand so gently in his. In his half-lidded, intense gaze. But he looked . . . normal. In love.

Chantal returned with a glass of ice water. "You okay?"

"I will be one day, I hope." I sipped, the cold water numbing the roof of my mouth. "You don't have to babysit me. You can go home."

"No way am I leaving right now." She sat in the armchair next to the couch, adjusted her bracelet. Kieran sat in that chair when we entertained. Sprawled out, arms and legs open to indicate command of a room. He could hold guests enthralled with his erudite ramblings about history, politics, medicine.

The man could put on a show. I just didn't know he'd been doing it with me, the whole time.

I got up, teetered a little as I put my glass of water on the table. Chantal jumped up to hold on to my arm, the stones clacking on her bracelet. She wore so many quartz crystals, she seemed more like a fortune-teller than a computer whiz. "You need to go to the clinic," she said. "I'll drive you."

"I'm not stepping into the same building with Kieran. I'm fine."

"You don't look fine."

"That's because I caught him in bed with another woman." There, I'd said it. I sat back down and exhaled.

She fell back into the armchair. "Wow. Seriously? They were actually—"

"Naked in bed. Yes."

She touched the stones on her necklace and swallowed. "He sure knew how to fool you." Her gaze drifted up to the wedding photo.

A hollow space opened inside me, a deep well of grief. "He's an actor as well as a liar." All his words of love, the emotion in his blue eyes—had it all been spun from silk? I picked up my water glass again, swirling the ice inside. The cubes were in the shapes of tiny whales—the ice tray had been a gift from Kieran for my birthday.

She wrinkled her nose. "No wonder you fainted. That's a lot to take. I don't know what to say."

"No need to say anything. I don't need sympathy."

"Who was it? Diane Jasper, wasn't it? The home stager?"

I nodded. "How did you know?"

She looked out the window, then back at me. "I was going to tell you. I saw the same Prius parked on the main road yesterday, just around the corner. Nobody ever parks there. I thought it was weird. Then I saw her walking through the woods toward your house. I don't think she saw me out on the trail. She went to the back door and knocked, and then someone opened the door and she went inside."

"Someone."

"It must've been Kieran. I was too far away to tell for sure. I thought it was odd."

My heart plummeted. "They were so sneaky. All for what? So that if you or someone else happened to stop by, there would be no other car in the driveway?"

"They were careful," she said. "Or so they thought."

I tried to imagine the deception, a woman traipsing through the woods to meet my husband, to sleep with him. "Doesn't she have any morals? No sense of guilt?" I could feel the tears springing to my eyes. "Just coming over like that, sneaking around?"

Chantal flipped her hair over her shoulder again. She flexed the ropy muscles in her forearms. She had once entered triathlons; now she took long runs in the woods. "It takes two to tango," she said firmly. "Kieran has to open the door, let her in, and do all the rest of it."

"I know," I said angrily. "But why would he risk everything? Why bother to marry me? Why would she do such a thing, knowing he's married?"

"He did it because he could, because you weren't supposed to be home yet," Chantal said, pointing a finger at me. "And she did it because women do horrible things to hurt each other sometimes. She's infatuated with him. Kieran is cute; he's a doctor. Face it, he's got the charm. You know, the way he kind of looks at you sideways, smiles a little like he's thinking something naughty . . ." She stared off vaguely.

"He never looked at you that way, did he?" I said, sitting up straight. "I didn't notice him looking at women that way."

"Oh, he gave me the eye once in a while," she said, pretending to pick lint off her T-shirt. "I ignored it. Just a glance now and then."

"And you didn't tell me."

"People flirt—usually it's harmless. I didn't see any reason to mention it." Chantal moved onto the couch next to me, and I scooted away from her.

"Did you flirt with him?"

"Hell no. I wouldn't do that!" She played with the crystals on her bracelet. "Besides, I'm still getting over Bill."

"You've been divorced—"

"Almost two years now."

I smoothed down my sweater, held up my left hand, and looked at my ring finger, the gold engraving glinting in the light. "Tomorrow's our anniversary," I said. "We were supposed to go sailing this weekend. He mentioned showing me a secluded beach on one of the islands."

Chantal reached out to pat my arm. "I'm so sorry—at least you found out now that he's not the man for you."

"He and Diane deserve each other," I said bitterly. But inside I was reeling—I could still see Kieran reaching out to touch my cheek. Coming home with vanilla cake for my birthday. An accumulation of memories, blowing away like dust. "He said it was an impulsive thing, but if you saw her here yesterday . . ."

"He's a planner. Last time you threw a dinner party, he was talking about specific travel routes he had all mapped out for the two of you, remember? To Australia, Bali, Paris? I'm willing to bet—"

"He planned this before I left."

"Most likely." Chantal pushed her hair back behind her ear. "And we all thought he was so . . . loyal. Our whole family loved going to see him. Even Jenny, and she hated doctors."

"You don't have to stop seeing him on my account."

"He was good to Jenny." She looked at me, her eyes bright with tears. "It's her birthday next week—did I tell you?" She sat beside me again, another whiff of floral perfume hitting my nose.

"No," I said, touching her hand. "How old would she have been?"

"Twenty. Can you believe it?" Chantal twisted her crystal bracelet around and around. "Four years gone, just like that. My baby girl would be a college sophomore now, driving for years. She was just getting her learner's permit . . ." She stared blankly at the wall.

"I'm so sorry," I said, squeezing her fingers.

"Yeah, well. I should move away, but I can't abandon her spirit, you know?" She shook her head slowly. "Bill had the right idea, leaving me. And Nick's even farther away in Korea—he's still teaching. So no husband, no son. But look at me, bending your ear."

"It's all right," I said. "Misery loves company."

"Anything I can do? I could plant a virus in the clinic computers."

I smiled wanly. "Thanks for the offer, but I don't want to harm Kieran's patients."

"We could target only his laptop. Where is it?"

"Probably at the farmhouse or the office."

"I could mess with Diane's computer, too."

"I don't know if she even has one. I don't know anything about her," I said, trying not to picture her leaping out of bed, breasts jiggling. I wished I had not seen her naked—now I would never be able to erase the image from my mind. Kieran had touched her with the same hands that had touched me. My insides were twisting, a blistering rage in my blood.

Chantal glanced nervously at the knife on the floor. "You might want to put that away."

"Right, my murder weapon of choice." *Maybe I should've used it,* I thought. I could've surprised Diane and Kieran in the throes of passion, stabbed them to death before they'd even known what was happening. I was surprised at how satisfying the images were to me, of their gaping wounds, of the blood seeping out across the sheets.

CHAPTER FOUR

After Chantal left, I grabbed Diane's lacy bra off the towel rack. Size 32D, front closure, reeking of sandalwood. I tossed the slip of fabric into a donation bag for the thrift shop. Then I stuffed the bedsheets into the wash, unpacked my suitcase, hung up the clean clothes I had not worn in the city, threw the dirty ones into the laundry basket. When devastated, perform useless, mundane tasks to keep from jumping off a cliff. Not that there was a cliff nearby.

The conversation between Kieran and Diane kept looping through my head. *Wish she could just be gone already . . .* She must have meant she wanted Kieran to file for divorce and, what, kick me out of my own house? I would be the one to file for divorce. They would be gone, the both of them, as far from me as possible.

I want it to be done, Diane had said. What had she wanted done? The divorce? Their sneaking around? A specific plan she imagined had been set in motion?

Patience . . . You have to learn to play the long game. Kieran's replies made me shiver. What was the long game? It was crazy to think he would want to, what, kill me? But we were supposed to go sailing over the weekend—he could've been planning to throw me overboard.

No, impossible. I was still in shock, my mind racing in crazy directions. Maybe he'd meant to come clean, to tell me about the affair. Or was he seriously planning to leave me for her?

I sat on the edge of the bed, doubled over again, a cramping in my abdomen. This couldn't be happening—I tried to rewind to our blissful moments. His gentle kiss on my neck, from a place of genuine love. *She came on to me . . . I love you.* What if he meant it? What if he did regret his mistake?

No, it didn't matter. His actions, what he'd done—that was what mattered. And what he had done could never be forgiven. *Stop looping on this,* I admonished myself, getting up. I went down to the kitchen to make a calming tea blend, watching the kettle steam, rattle, and then whistle shrilly as the water boiled. I couldn't stop my hands from shaking.

I could cancel the rest of my appointments . . . We could fuck all afternoon. I wanted to unhear his words, gouge them out of my ears. Sever his vocal cords. Silence him. These violent thoughts weren't normal, I knew, but then nothing about this day had been normal. He and Diane had not been normal lovers engaging in normal adultery. They hadn't said, *Come to me, baby. I want you. I need you.* No, he'd said, *Patience. Chill out . . . the long game.*

I'd kept pouring into my mug, the hot water overflowing onto the countertop, like a wound bleeding out. Blinking back to reality, I wiped up the water, tossed the tea leaves into the compost bin. I had to tamp down my rising nausea, keep my head on straight.

I thought of confronting Diane, demanding to know exactly what she'd meant. Perhaps she would be honest with me, if Kieran wouldn't. Or did I even care? I didn't want to give them the time of day. I felt violated, befouled, duped—and embarrassed. Of all the ways to discover the emptiness of my marriage, I'd been subjected to the sleaziest, most clichéd kind of humiliation.

And I'd told Chantal all about it. She was not a gossip, but I regretted spilling my guts to her. What if the news were to leak out? *Clueless Wife Discovers Unfaithful Doctor Husband in Sordid Affair With His Mistress . . .*

No matter what he had done, I would look like the fool to have been so blind. I didn't care what anyone on the island thought, did I? But I had to live here. I had to shop at the co-op, run my business. Interact with my neighbors. It mattered what they thought, but then, if they were going to gossip about me, were they really my friends, anyway? I couldn't be concerned about what might leak out into the community.

I didn't want anything of Kieran's in my sight. He was out of here. I began throwing his clothes into his large suitcase, and when the suitcase was full, I stuffed garbage bags. I had half a mind to let the waste management truck pick them up, but I dumped everything downstairs by the front door.

In the dining room, on top of the liquor cabinet, I found two tumblers next to his most expensive whisky, a Glenlivet single malt. So I emptied the bottle in the kitchen sink. Five hundred bucks down the drain. Along with the rest of his pretentious collection. Bon voyage. I dropped the empty bottles into the recycling bin, proud of my achievement.

Then I bagged the supplies and the anniversary gifts I'd bought in Seattle and took them outside to the shop. I would sell them or maybe even give them away. Along the garden path, I slowed through fragrant lavender beds, fennel stalks, lemon balm, and patches of mint. The odorless white flowers of fern-leaf dropwort made an excellent tea for treating rheumatoid arthritis. But what herb could heal a shattered heart?

A strangely shaped plant had reemerged in the herb bed, the reddish flowers themselves resembling tiny hearts. The Juliet. My mother had brought back cuttings and seeds from South America many years earlier and had not been able to identify the species—so she had named it herself. Juliet had been her middle name. Selene Juliet Watters.

Somehow, the plant kept volunteering in the garden, sprouting every couple of years in a new spot. Perhaps birds deposited the seeds. My mother had used the powdered extract in tinctures and formulas, but she had always warned me not to touch the plant. She had once told me the story of a client whose husband had died after ingesting too much of the extract in my mother's Slumber powder, although the official cause of death had been a heart attack. *No substances were found in his system, but I knew better,* my mother had said. *I told her to give him only two teaspoons. She must've given him the whole bag. She must've killed him, but nobody ever knew—and I couldn't prove it if anyone asked.*

The story had unsettled me. I didn't know if it was true, but I did know that seemingly benign plants could have toxic properties. Tulip bulbs could cause skin irritation if handled for too long without gloves. The large-leafed angel's trumpet dangling over the path could make the eyes dilate if sniffed, and ingestion would likely be fatal. I loved rhubarb, but the large leaves were high in oxalic acid, which could quickly cause kidney failure in humans.

I imagined Kieran and Diane munching on rhubarb leaves or angel's trumpet or biting into toxic foxglove or larkspur. A salad of any number of poisonous shrubs would do, the way I was thinking. Garnished with deadly nightshade. It would take only a few of its bright red berries to kill an adult.

At the threshold to the Clary Sage, I wiped my feet on the mat. The shopfront was a hexagon, sashed windows on four sides, the sashed door in front. The sixth side was the back wall of the shop opening to the prep room. The effect was a panoply of lights reflecting off the many squares of glass. The door was unlocked. *Kieran must've come out here while I was away,* I thought with a stab of annoyance. He had a key—I would have to get it back from him.

Inside, my shop had been disturbed. The aromatherapy sprays, tins of tea leaves, and herbal tinctures were all still artfully displayed, but small things were amiss. A tea towel had been unfolded. And the soaps had been rearranged in the dishes. I had placed vintage apothecary bottles in strategic locations on the shelves, but one had been moved to the windowsill. I would have the locks changed, and Kieran would never be allowed back in here. I hated the idea that Diane might've been in here touching everything.

I'd bought a vintage amber bottle in the city, with a cork stopper, labeled Magnesii Oxidum Ponderosum. I placed it next to the clear bottle on the windowsill, which still had its original label reading Poison. But I didn't know what the bottle had originally contained. The label listing the contents had long ago worn off.

My mother had made her formulas in the prep room, which now also showed signs of disturbance. The front row of her clothbound journals, on the shelf behind the prep table, had tipped over.

"What do you think, Mom?" I said to her photograph smiling from the wall. Her golden eyes gazed at me wisely, black hair spilling to her waist. "Did Kieran and Diane come in here and mess around?"

Her smile seemed to falter a little. Now I better understood why she had never remarried after my father's death. Perhaps one heartbreak had been enough. But he hadn't meant to hurt her. When the car accident had claimed him in Mission Canyon, he'd been on his way home to her with a dozen roses on the passenger seat. Her grief had run so deep, she had fled California, whisking me north to Chinook Island, where a college friend had run a bed-and-breakfast. I'd been only a year old when my mother had bought this blue Victorian and the cottage with a fraction of the funds my dad had left her. She'd had no inkling of his wealth. When she'd met him in the Santa Barbara Botanic Garden, he'd been working as a groundskeeper. He'd kept his money a secret, preferring an ordinary life. He'd been a gentle and kind man, from all accounts, and after I was born, he was reportedly happy to dote on me, rocking me, singing to me, and telling me stories before I could understand the words.

She had kept his surname rather than reverting to her maiden name, Clary—except to name her shop the Clary Sage. And I'd never taken Kieran's surname, lucky for me. I was still conveniently Elise Watters, not Elise Lund.

I placed the gifts I'd bought for Kieran on display shelves, priced the items, and then locked up the shop and called him from the driveway, where my cell phone caught a signal. He answered right away. I didn't know where he was, and I didn't care. "Why the hell did you go into my shop?"

"I didn't," he said. "I swear."

"Well, someone was in there!"

"Yeah," he said, lowering his voice. "It was you."

"It was not me. I've been away for three days."

"You were in there the morning before you left. Don't you remember? Early. You were in your pajamas."

I held the phone away from my head, then pressed it to my ear again. "You're a liar."

"It's the truth. I looked out the bedroom window and saw you coming out of there. Before sunrise. You came back to bed. I asked you if everything was all right. You just mumbled and went back to sleep."

"You're so full of shit."

"Look, I have to go. We have to talk about this later."

I hung up, headed back into the main house. How could I believe anything he ever told me? He'd stopped short of suggesting I'd been sleepwalking. I'd told him about my previous episodes, during the traumatic last days of my first marriage, and about my mother's occasional bouts of somnambulating when I was a child.

But I had no memory of going into the shop the morning I'd left for the city. I'd woken in bed, gone straight to catch the ferry. No, I couldn't believe anything Kieran said. I needed to reclaim his key to my shop, right now. He'd left his entire set of keys somewhere in the house, probably on the foyer table.

But they weren't there. I checked under the pile of mail. Then I glimpsed the keys on the floor behind a bookshelf next to the entryway. They must've fallen. I got down on my hands and knees and retrieved the key ring, to which he had attached a black caduceus monogrammed disk showing two serpents in a double helix around the wand of Hermes. A medical symbol of rebirth and regeneration, but the Greek god Hermes also protected thieves and liars. *How apt,* I thought.

The metal car key on the ring opened Kieran's old Jaguar. The brass keys to our house and the shop were also on the ring, as well as a silver Schlage key to his farmhouse. I removed the key to the shop and tucked it into my pocket.

There were two smaller, identical keys, a double set for a lockbox, a safe, or maybe a filing cabinet.

Filing cabinet.

He'd moved two metal ones in here from his farmhouse. They were now in the alcove between the dining room and the library. I went down the hall to the alcove. Books were piled on his desk, on the shelves. One filing cabinet was unlocked, empty. The other was locked.

An envelope sat on the desk next to the filing cabinet, addressed to Kieran. The envelope had been sliced open with the letter opener. I pulled out a folded slip of paper, a credit card bill with a $5,000 balance. Not unusual, if he'd bought equipment for the clinic. But still a startling amount. The bill had been delivered to a post office box, which struck me as strange. I'd been with him when he'd filled out the address-change form to have his mail forwarded here.

What else had been delivered to the post office box? And where was the mail now? I'd seen him casually slipping papers into the filing cabinet. As if it were nothing. But the husband I thought I'd known was now treacherous, unmapped terrain.

I hesitated, but not for long. He had forfeited his privacy, as far as I was concerned. I slid one of the matching small keys into the lock in the cabinet—it fit. The locking mechanism turned easily. It was cheap. I could've broken in with a screwdriver, I supposed. But Kieran had never expected me to try.

I opened the drawer, flipped through manila file folders marked "Insurance," "Dental," "Home Value," "Repair," and so on. Boring, the usual paper trail of a life. But in the very back, an unmarked manila file folder had been so tightly wedged in, I had to remove other files to extract it.

I closed the drawer, sat in the swiveling chair at his desk, and opened the file. Inside were student loan statements, presumably for medical school. The active balances were eye-popping. There were hospital bills for amounts not covered by insurance for his ex-wife's emergency care when she had died of flu complications. And more credit card bills for several different accounts, all of which he had run up to their limits. He appeared to be making minimum payments.

That was by no means all. He owed a substantial mortgage for the farmhouse, payments for the boat, his old Jaguar, and several thousand dollars for an Eames armchair. The indulgence, especially in the face of his other debts, made me sick to my stomach.

The papers blurred—the walls receded. I felt like an idiot. But this was all only paper. What if he hid more from me in his laptop computer, in the proverbial internet cloud? He'd stuck with paper delivered to his secret post office box in town, but for all I knew, he had more debts that weren't here in the file.

I stuffed the file folder back in its place, closed and locked the drawer, pounded my fists on top of the cabinet until my hand hurt. I'd indulged him in gifts "for the man who has everything." An expensive silk pocket square, a chronograph watch, a high-end camera. I'd admired his ability to graciously accept them. He didn't need to be in control, the man providing for his wife in a traditional sense, as

Brandon had always wanted to be. Brandon had not appreciated gifts from me. I'd thought Kieran was more comfortable in the world, more self-possessed, but now I understood that he was materialistic. At the very least.

Our recent, brief phone call, on my drive home from the ferry, snaked back into my mind. *So the meeting with the adviser went well?* He'd urged me to see my financial adviser in the first place. *Ready to trade in the Honda?* Kieran, preoccupied with expensive, fast cars. *Look at that Lamborghini. My midlife crisis car?* he'd once joked. Maybe it hadn't been a joke.

He'd paid extra attention to the balances in my investment accounts, opened the statements when they arrived in the mail, made sure I updated the beneficiary information. *Looks like your index fund performed well last quarter,* he'd said a few weeks earlier, before opening a bottle of wine to celebrate. *I love you so much. Have you thought of investing in a more aggressive growth fund?* I'd chalked it up to his interest in finance, a topic that made my eyes glaze over.

But his motivations might have been more sinister. I was worth nearly $5 million, and he knew it. He needed my money. Why hadn't I been more alert to this possibility? I'd been grieving the loss of my mother, leaning on Kieran for support. Even now, his charming smile, his deep voice, his careful attention to my needs—it had all become a part of me. I still couldn't believe what was happening. I thought I could snap my fingers, click my heels together, and I would be home again, like Dorothy returning from Oz, back in the life I thought we'd shared, perfect and beautiful and full of love. I couldn't comprehend that I'd fallen—or had almost fallen—victim to his greed. But now what mattered most was what I was going to do about it.

CHAPTER FIVE

Out in the driveway, I scrolled through the contacts on my cell phone until I reached the listing for my business attorney, Gabe Harvell. He'd been my mother's attorney, too. I could picture him in his San Juan Island office overlooking Friday Harbor. The model airplanes on his shelves next to his law textbooks. The photographs of his family on his desk, next to crayon pictures his granddaughter had drawn for him. I called his number, got his voice mail.

"I'm out of the office in litigation proceedings," he said. "Please leave a message and I'll return your call when I am able."

When he is able. "I need to update my will immediately," I said, trying to keep my voice calm. "I need to lock out my husband, please. Call me back."

Lock out. I hung up, returned to the house, fell into another crying jag. Exhausted, I forced myself to heat up a frozen dinner, but my stomach couldn't handle much. Outside the window, a movement in the garden caught my eye. Dusk was falling. I turned on the porch light and flung open the door to the cold air. "Hello? Is anyone out here?" There was a rustling in the woods, then quiet. *Probably a deer or a raccoon,* I thought, but it spooked me to be here alone.

Back inside, I locked all the doors and windows and staggered up to bed. It was too late, and I was too tired to make any more decisions.

But I couldn't bear to return to the master bedroom, where I had seen Kieran with Diane, and I hadn't remade the bed after ripping off all the sheets. So I moved into my childhood room, with its view of the front garden. In this cozy space, my mother had read to me, brought me soup when I was sick, lifted my spirits. I missed her tonight with a deep ache, wished I could consult with her about what to do.

I twisted off my gold wedding band and threw it as hard as I could. It cracked against the wall, bounced off, and pinged to the floor. I didn't bother to pick it up. I knew I was being dramatic, but I had a right. *I'm going to be dramatic all over the place,* I thought. But I was soon asleep.

Kieran came to me in a dream, slipped into bed beside me. We were fine. We were whole again. Nothing bad had happened. He took my hand—all was well. He kissed me softly on the lips. I felt an incredible sense of relief. I hadn't caught him in bed with Diane—it had all been a nightmare. We were happy, the breeze in my hair as we glided across the sea in his yacht. Then a gust of wind knocked me overboard, and I sank beneath the waves, swallowing water, suffocating. I struggled upward, a great weight on my chest. I tried to scream, but no sound came out. I could see Kieran's wavering silhouette above the surface, his arms pushing me down.

I jolted awake, gasping in the dim light of dawn. Someone stood in the doorway, a vague silhouette. I shot upright, my heart hammering, and backed up against the headboard. I fumbled for the lamp on the nightstand, a weapon. "Who are you? What do you want? Get out of here!"

"You're so beautiful when you sleep," Kieran said placidly, switching on the ceiling light. I squinted in the sudden brightness, let go of the lamp.

"How did you get in?" I was still half in the dream, underwater, shielding my eyes against the light.

"Sorry." He switched off the bright overhead light, reached over to turn on the soft bedside lamp instead. "Is that better?"

"What are you doing here?" I repeated, peering at him in the bluish lamplight.

"I came home to be with my wife."

"What?" My breath caught. How could he be here again? After I'd threatened him with a butcher knife? "I told you to leave."

"I know you didn't mean it. I can't stop thinking about you." He was in sweats and running shoes. He sat at the edge of the bed. I felt the mattress depressing beneath me.

"You're trespassing," I snapped, fully awake now. "You can't just—"

"I like to watch you sleep. Looked like you were having a bad dream. I almost woke you."

I shivered, wondering if he had "almost" smothered me with a pillow. A cold draft of air seeped in from somewhere. "How long were you standing in the doorway?"

"Long enough." He smiled. "I can't believe you're in this little room—"

"How did you get into the house?" I pulled the covers up to my neck. "I thought you left your keys."

"I did." He pulled a single spare key from the pocket of his sweatpants. "I always keep another one under a stone."

"You didn't tell me," I said, my heart racing. My emotions were at war—part of me was relieved to see him; another part of me was somehow terrified of him.

"I thought you knew," he said gently. "I told you. The key is under the white rock next to the path by the front door."

"No, you didn't tell me."

"I did, six months ago."

Had he told me, or was he lying again? "There are quite a few rocks in the garden," I said, my voice shaky.

"I showed you which one."

"No, you didn't." I tried to remember. I reached for the glass of water I kept by the bed at night, gulped down the liquid. I felt parched, the dream still vivid in my mind. "How long were you standing in the doorway? Really?"

"Not long." But I had the strange feeling he'd been watching me, silently, for a while. He looked around the room, at my shelves of books from childhood, my stuffed animals lined up on the shelves. My mother had never thrown anything away. He gestured toward the hall. "I called for you when I came in, but you didn't answer, so I went up to our room."

"My room. It's not yours anymore." I would've heard his voice—he must not have called for me at all. Or maybe I'd been in a deep sleep.

"Diane was the one who wanted to come here," he said, his voice still soft. "I didn't want to—she told me she wanted to see the garden for inspiration. She's working in her dad's garden—"

"You should've said no. You should not have gone anywhere with her!"

"You need to understand what happened. I'm human—couples deal with this kind of thing all the time."

"I don't care what other couples deal with."

"Don't you remember what day this is?" His face fell in disappointment.

"I know what day it is," I said, hardly able to catch my breath. "We're not celebrating."

"Do you remember the way we danced?" His voice dropped to almost a whisper.

"Of course I remember," I said, making my voice harsh to hold off the pain. We'd danced after the wedding guests had left and the music had ended, our arms wrapped tightly around each other. Other happy moments flowed through me—evenings spent dancing in the dark, our trips on the ferry, the time we'd been out on the windy deck, watching orcas breaching in the strait. I saw him bringing me breakfast in bed in Maui on our honeymoon. Interlacing his fingers with mine, insisting on holding my hand on our hikes, even if the trail was only wide enough for one person. At night, his presence had been a comfort, his arm wrapped around my waist as we spooned. But now the memories fell over like building blocks. I longed to see him the way I had seen him before, as my loving husband.

"Don't ever forget the good times. I won't," he said sadly. "We can go back to the way things were."

"No, we can't!" But I wanted to. Oh, how I wanted to, but everything was befouled now. Ruined. I didn't know the man sitting at the foot of my single bed, staring at me with an expression I could not identify.

He reached into his pocket, handed me a small velvet box. "I went to Seattle to get these for you last month," he said. "Remember when I had that medical conference? Happy anniversary."

I didn't take the box from him, so he laid it on the bedcover. He could've taken Diane to the city with him, for all I knew. I wished him an anniversary in hell. "I don't want it," I said.

"Open it," he said, nodding toward the velvet box.

"No, take it back, whatever it is. You need to leave." I'd bought him a shirt, a handmade English shaving brush, a pair of wool socks, all down in the cottage. I wasn't going to give them to him. Ever.

"I live here," he said. "We need to talk."

"No, we don't. There's nothing to say. And you don't live here, not anymore."

"You know I do." He reached for me, but I snatched my hand away, tucked it under the covers.

"If you want to see me next time, call first," I said. "It's the crack of dawn."

"I'm always up early, you know that. I was out for a run along the harbor. And we have plans."

"What?" I said, incredulous. "We don't have any more plans, ever." How could he come in here, sit at the end of my bed, hand me a gift, after everything that had happened? Did he really believe what he'd done didn't matter?

"The best thing would be for us to go on our trip and try to work this out," he said, touching my arm. I flinched.

"On our trip? You still want to go sailing? Are you crazy?"

"We have hotel reservations—I was going to sail us into Salmon Bay Marina—"

"Stop!" I said, holding up my hands. I squeezed my eyes shut, opened them. "Just. Stop. Why are you acting like nothing has happened?" I flung off the covers, got out of bed, slid my feet into my slippers. They felt slightly damp inside.

"Because it wasn't anything. It was nothing to me."

"To *you*. You're . . . unbelievable." I went down the hall, through the master bedroom to the bathroom. He followed me, watching me in the mirror from the doorway as I brushed my teeth.

"You're so beautiful," he said.

I looked at myself—I felt far from beautiful, with my puffy eyes, my splotchy cheeks, my tangle of dark hair. He'd said the same thing many times. I'd always felt as if he spoke the truth. I'd always felt beautiful when he'd said I was beautiful. But now his words rang hollow. A wall of protection went up inside me. I washed and dried my face. I was bristling. "What game are you playing? Do you think if you just sweet-talk me and diminish what happened, I'll come around?"

"I'm not pretending it didn't happen, but don't you think you're overreacting? It's over."

"Yes, our marriage is over, exactly!"

"No, I mean I broke things off with Diane—I'm not going to see her again."

"You should not have started 'things' in the first place."

"I told you, it's done. I'm back here one hundred percent. With you."

"Well, I'm one hundred percent done with you. You can't just come in here like this."

His eyes went flat, as if all the blue had been drained out of them. "You can't stop me," he said quietly.

I stopped cold at the bedroom closet, in the middle of pulling a sweater off its hanger. "What did you say?" I said, turning to face him. Time slowed again. I saw the way things had happened, the ghost of Diane behind him, scrambling out of bed. Kieran, naked, trying to explain. It was as if he'd completely forgotten. Here he was, in the house again after I'd almost stabbed him. The nerve. But his expression was mild, passive. "I said, you can't stop me. I'm not giving up. I'm your husband." His voice was still soft and even.

"I'm filing for divorce." My voice shook. I tried to pass him on the way to the door, but he grabbed my wrist, his grip so tight I thought my bone would snap.

"No," he said. "I don't want a divorce."

"You're hurting me," I said, yanking my arm away.

"Sorry. I'm sorry. Talk to me. I can't lose you." In the shadows, his face looked angular, malevolent.

"You mean, you can't lose my money."

"What?" He blinked at me, as if he really didn't comprehend.

"Your debts. You left an envelope here from your post office box, and—"

"Shit." He ran his fingers through his hair, sat on the edge of the master bed.

"Yes, shit. I opened your filing cabinet."

He looked up at me sharply. "You found my keys."

"No," I lied, but I could feel myself blushing. "You left the cabinet unlocked."

He nodded slightly, ran his hand down his face, a bead of sweat on his forehead. "So you know my situation."

"I know your situation very well, yes." I strode past him to the stairs, and he followed me down.

"You're not going to come at me with a knife again, are you?"

"Only if you stay here."

"Come on." He followed me into the kitchen, watched me pour water into the coffee maker. "I was going to tell you."

"When?" I shouted. "Next year? The year after?"

"I'm paying my bills," he said, pacing.

"Good for you. You and . . . Diane can finish paying them off together." I scooped coffee grounds into the basket.

"Do you know what it's like when you graduate from medical school? You get any amount of credit you want. You get approved for loans. You think you're going to stay on top of everything, but it's impossible. And when Lana got sick, we got into more debt, and I couldn't work my way out of it."

"Your ex-wife."

"Ask anyone, Elise. I'm not the only physician up to his ears in obligations."

I opened the fridge, brought out the soy milk. He was making a dent in my certainty. "But you lied!"

"I was embarrassed!" he shouted, his cheeks flushed. "Being in debt—it wasn't a crime. It was a bad choice."

"Seems you made a number of bad choices," I said, bringing a mug down from the cabinet.

He pulled the velvet box out from his pocket again, placed it on the countertop next to me. So he'd brought it downstairs. "Open it."

I looked at the box, sighed. "Really, I can't."

"Fine, I'll open it for you." He flipped up the top of the box to reveal a pair of delicate, hand-carved silver earrings featuring teardrop images of orcas. I'd coveted those earrings at Pike Place Market in Seattle the last time we'd visited the city together. I felt a tiny corner of my heart softening, but then it hardened again.

"Thank you for being so thoughtful. But I can't accept them. They don't make up for what you have done."

"I know that," he said, sliding the box across the counter. "Keep them anyway. I love you. I'll do anything for you. We can go to therapy. You can put a tracker on my phone."

"Stop it," I said, my voice breaking. "Don't you understand? I shouldn't have to do such a thing."

"I know. Look. Talk to Diane. She'll tell you I broke it off—that I won't ever see her again."

"What about the next time?"

"There won't be a next time!"

"Stop!" I slammed my hand on the countertop, and he fell instantly quiet. "Stop going on and on, trying to wear me down. It's not going to work. Get the hell out." I turned to glare up at him, and his eyes had darkened, as if clouds moved inside them.

"All right," he said quietly. "But this isn't the end, and you know it. Not over some small mistake, a blip—a slipup. You don't let anyone be human, Elise. You don't let anyone make human mistakes. You're a perfectionist like your mother."

"Like my mother!" I shouted. "She wasn't—"

"Well, I have news for you. I'm not perfect, and neither are you. I see the way you look at your ex-husband every time he's in town."

"What?" I shouted, my jaw nearly coming unhinged. "His projects here have nothing to do with me."

"Oh yeah?" He raised his voice, gaining steam. "He's back again. I've seen him. And now he's building a deck for Chantal. You know why? He wants to be close to you, that's why." He jabbed his forefinger in the direction of Chantal's house. His words threw me off-balance.

"I . . . didn't know he was working for her," I said, as the coffee began to percolate. "He did work for my mother—it's not surprising that she would have referred him to—"

"I thought he built mansions for tech CEOs."

"He does, but his guys do the work. He has employees, foremen. He likes side projects. He likes helping people."

"Helping people. Is that what he's doing? More like, he makes up excuses to be on the island all the fucking time."

I frowned, a pain in my head. "How did this conversation get turned around?"

"It's not normal, Elise. He should stay in Seattle."

"It's normal for him to be here because he has built a reputation—"

"So you didn't know he was working right next door?"

"I really didn't know. And I don't even see him when he's here. Not intentionally. I mean, I run into him now and then." I looked toward Chantal's house, wondering how long Brandon had been working for her, why she hadn't mentioned it.

"Face it. The guy's still in love with you."

"We've been divorced three years."

"He doesn't care! Do you really think he comes here to build houses? He comes here to try to get you back."

"Now you're being ridiculous," I said, shaking my head. "I can't believe you would come in here again and lay this on me, try to make me feel like I'm responsible—"

"Fine. I'll go for now, but I'll be back. I need my keys."

"I haven't seen them," I lied, staring out in the direction of Chantal's house, dense forest obscuring the view.

He turned and strode into the front hall, and I followed, biting my tongue, withholding any mention of the keys hiding in my handbag. I wasn't sure why I didn't tell him I had them.

He gestured toward the suitcase and bags, turned to glare at me. "We need to talk about this. I live here."

"You have the farmhouse," I said. "I'm sure Diane would be happy to stay there with you. Is she really a home stager? Or was that part of the lie?"

"Yes, why wouldn't she be? She moved to the island a few months ago to take care of her dad. He was recovering from heart—"

"I don't need her life story. I would like to know how you met her, though. Did she come into your clinic?"

"Yes," he said reluctantly.

"How many other patients?"

"What? None! Elise, come on." He moved toward me, but I backed away, nearly tripping over a garbage bag full of clothes. He shook his head and sighed, then searched the table and the floor for his keys. He went upstairs, stomped around, came back down. "Let me know if you find them." He grabbed the handle of his suitcase and rolled it out to his car, returned for the garbage bags.

"Since you don't want to go on our trip today," he went on, "I've got patients who want to see me. We can still leave tomorrow. Or Sunday. I could take Monday and Tuesday off."

"Why, when your schedule is so crazy?" I said. "Oh, wait, you could cancel your appointments and fuck all afternoon. Or for the rest of your lives."

"Don't do this, Elise."

"Goodbye, Kieran." I slammed the door in his face, locked it, remembering only after he'd driven away that he still had his extra house key.

CHAPTER SIX

Chantal jogged down Lost Bluff Lane toward home. She wasn't winded—she was in better shape now than she had ever been. Every muscle well worked, accounted for, pumped to the limit. She passed Kieran's Jaguar traveling in the opposite direction, and her heart flipped. That fluttering pulse again. It happened whenever she saw him. Her reaction was like a reflex, uncontrollable, instant.

He'd obviously tried to go home, and Elise had kicked him out again. As was her way. Who knew what had gone on in that house? She had reason to be upset. Kieran had treated her like crap. Diane Jasper, seriously? The woman wasn't a woman. She was a girl.

Out of habit, Chantal raised her hand to wave at him, smiling briefly, as if she didn't know what was up. He waved back, and from this distance, she imagined his sad expression. He certainly did not flash his usual friendly grin.

She turned to watch the back of his car recede as he drove toward the stop sign at the corner, and she felt the familiar restlessness gnawing at her. He lingered there with the engine running, a plume of exhaust puffing from the tailpipe. She considered jogging over to talk to him, to offer a few neighborly words. She thought, in that moment, that he would turn left onto the main road and disappear, but instead he backed up, the white reverse lights on. She jogged forward, hearing her breathing, the swish of her jogging pants—her heart rate crazy fast the closer she got to him. She stopped in front of a dense thicket of trees, invisible from the blue Victorian. He backed up until she stood in line with the driver's-side door. Kieran rolled down the window. "Hey, how're you doing?"

"Morning." She gave him her most dazzling smile, aware that, after the treatments, her teeth looked whiter than ever. The sun was rising. She'd been out early, since before dawn, following the labyrinth of pathways through the woods, using a small flashlight to illuminate the trail. "How are things?"

He nodded back toward the house. "You saw what happened yesterday—"

"Oh, yesterday." She waved her arm dismissively, pretending she didn't care that she'd seen him outside in only his coat, getting into Diane's Prius, that she had not found Elise passed out on the floor, next to a gleaming knife. "I meant today."

"Things are better," he said. "You know how she gets."

"How she gets?"

He tapped his fingers on the steering wheel. "Elise has been depressed. I worry about her." But Chantal could feel his attention shifting to her body. She could always tell.

"So do I."

"I need to get her into therapy before she does something stupid."

"Like what?" Chantal asked sharply. "She doesn't seem stupid to me."

"It's the way she's been feeling—her emotions are so extreme. Have you noticed?"

"I'll keep an eye out." Prickling, she glanced at her phone. "I should go. I'm expecting the contractor—"

"Brandon McLeod?" Kieran asked, staring at her.

"He's—you know he's working for me." She felt the blood rushing to her cheeks.

"Are you two, you know . . ."

"Dating?" she said. "Why do you want to know?"

Kieran shrugged. "No reason. You have a nice day."

As she watched him drive off, she wondered if she had detected a note of jealousy in his voice. If only he knew. The previous evening, Brandon had still been working on the deck at dusk when Elise had called Chantal's cell phone. A few minutes afterward, when Chantal had gone outside to check on him, she'd mentioned the call, told him that Elise and Kieran were having a little trouble. Brandon was good at masking his reactions, but the telltale scratching of his beard had indicated that he was irked. "Well, the guy was never right for her," he'd said, gathering up his tools. "See you tomorrow."

He would arrive soon, so she picked up her pace toward home. The faster she ran, the more she almost believed she could turn back time, like Superman when he'd soared around the earth, faster and faster, eventually spinning the planet backward, bringing Lois Lane back to life.

But Jenny would never come back. Her body was buried up at the cemetery, though her spirit still floated in the sea. When Chantal ran near the water, early in the mornings, she felt closer to her daughter.

She raced up the porch steps, two at a time, went straight into the kitchen to chug a tall glass of water. Her short conversation with Kieran had thrown her off, as talking to him always did. She wasn't herself around him. He had seemed interested. But then there was Elise, Diane. Did she want to go there?

Next to the sink, Jenny's ceramic bird was on display, the one she'd made in first-grade art class. The little bird had two bug eyes facing forward, a predator with binocular vision. Every minute of Jenny's life was now hardened into a similar ceramic glaze, unchangeable, all potential thwarted. She would never fulfill her dream of becoming a sculptor. She would never travel the world, never get married, never have children of her own. Never grow old.

Chantal found herself wiping away tears as she popped bread into the toaster, went through the motions of making breakfast. Even after all these years—four years that felt like forever and like no time at all—she cried almost daily.

She should have understood the signs. *I should have done more,* she thought, although everyone had assured her that there was nothing she could have done. *I should have made sure she didn't miss her psychotherapy appointments. I should have asked her more questions. I should have paid better attention to where she went and with whom.*

Maybe she should do something more now, for Elise, but what? She considered going back to check on her neighbor, but what would she say? That she'd been out before dawn, spying? That she had seen a light on in the Clary Sage, had jogged up the side spur on the trail for a better look inside? That front room was like a fishbowl, the light blazing out. She'd seen Elise in the prep room, barefoot, in pajamas. Weighing powder on the scale, her eyes half-closed.

It had been startling. Unsure what to do, Chantal had crouched out of view, watching. Jenny had been a sleepwalker as a child. When Chantal and Bill had tried to wake her, she had screamed and pummeled them with her fists. Nick, their eldest, had slept through it all, out like a light every night. Now he would probably never return home from Seoul. He loved Korea, loved teaching. He didn't like to speak of Jenny, didn't like to be reminded of her.

Bill and Chantal had taken her to a psychologist for the sleepwalking—and they were advised not to try to wake her again. Sleepwalkers did not know the people they loved and could not recognize faces.

But they also couldn't perform complicated tasks that required higher cognitive functions. Which was why sleepwalkers rarely got dressed, and if they did, they put on strange clothes—whatever was handy—or walked outside in their pajamas or naked. They spoke gibberish, and since they were usually unaware of their environment, they were prone to tripping and falling or hurting themselves.

But people got up and walked in the night for other reasons, too. They weren't always asleep. They could be on drugs, or drunk, or performing higher functions on automatic, almost as if hypnotized. And they wouldn't remember anything afterward.

Chantal thought Elise must've fallen into that category, in an altered state, either drunk or on drugs or simply experiencing a weird mental glitch. Her eyes were still half-closed as she'd made a powdered mess. Chantal had decided not to try to wake her.

Jenny had outgrown her somnambulism, but obviously Elise had not. She had wiped the table, walked to the door, turned off the light, and stepped outside. She had wandered into the garden, had not seen Chantal in the shadows. Then she had gone back into the house and had closed the door.

Chantal had lingered a minute, trying to decide what to do. She'd opted to let things be. She'd gone on her way, jogging back down the spur trail to the beach, then looping up onto the main road toward Lost Bluff Lane. As she'd picked up her pace, a plan had begun to form in her mind. Now, as she spread peanut butter on toast, the details of her plan coalesced.

Since Bill had moved out, she hadn't felt desirable, if she were honest. His departure had been a blow to her self-esteem. But he'd been an idiot to abandon the marriage—his loss. She was fun and smart. She was good company. She had assets. And men still looked at her, rubbernecking as they passed in cars, when she was out for her run. Kieran was no exception. She would invest in a new, sexy wardrobe, maybe a lacy G-string from the lingerie boutique in town. Have her hair styled, buy shiny lipstick. She knew she was attractive, but she needed to make herself absolutely irresistible.

CHAPTER SEVEN

After Kieran left, I dumped out the coffee and made a pot of herbal tea to calm my nerves. I was jumpy, and my stomach had not been behaving lately. As I sipped from my mug, I considered my options. I thought about how I'd woken to see him looking at me from the bedroom doorway, and I shivered again. Strange, the way it had seemed so normal, wonderful, in fact, to imagine him in this house with me, only a day earlier.

Now my rage festered. I'd dreamed he'd drowned me, for my money—and then there he had been, so placid, trying to pin the blame for our situation on me and my ex-husband. How long had he been nursing this paranoia about Brandon? I'd had no idea.

Brandon was working right next door. I needed to change the locks on the house, but there was no locksmith on Chinook Island. The locksmiths came over from the nearby islands. Brandon was a builder—and he knew how to change locks. He'd changed the locks on our house in Seattle.

Down the driveway again, I pulled up his contact information in my phone. The address where I had once lived in Seattle, the home telephone number that had once also been mine. But he wasn't there now. I supposed I'd been rude, not responding to his text when I'd first arrived home from the city, but we shared a troubled history. I still had his cell phone number on speed dial.

"Elise," he answered almost immediately, as if he'd been waiting for my call. His voice had a different tone from Kieran's—tenor instead of bass, but with a greater resonance, and he retained a slight twang from his upbringing in Houston.

"I'm sorry I haven't been in touch," I said. "I got your text—congratulations on your job on the island."

"Estate for a big tech CEO, the usual," he said. "So meet me for coffee?"

He always asked the same question, and I never replied directly. I thought of asking him if he was at Chantal's house, but it was really none of my business. "Um, could I ask you something? I'm going out on a limb here."

"Okay," he said, his voice cautious. "Fire away."

"Could you come to the house and change the locks?"

"You had a break-in?"

"Not exactly, but I might have one."

"Well, I might be able to—tomorrow?"

"No, I'm thinking right now. It's urgent."

"Right now. Is this a matter for the police, Elise? Because—"

"Can you do it? And not ask questions?"

"Nice to talk to you, too," he said, his voice rising in surprise.

"I'm sorry. I know I seem crazy."

"You're never crazy, Elise. But you sound scared. I need to stop at the hardware store, but okay. I can do it. Which doors? Front and back?"

"Yes, you know the house." He'd worked on it for my mother after our divorce, and he and I had spent nearly every holiday here with her. We'd decorated the living spruce tree in the front yard, and Brandon had been the one to string the Christmas lights along the eaves. "Could you do me a favor and not tell anyone you're doing this? Like, not my husband?"

"Why would I tell your husband?" Brandon sounded incredulous.

"Just, Brandon . . . please."

"Yeah, sure. I won't. I got it. I could be there in a few."

He arrived within the hour. When he got out of his truck, carrying a toolbox, at first I didn't recognize him. But when he got close, I knew him. Dark eyes, brooding and smoky. Thick brows, coal-colored beard and mustache. Clad in a flannel shirt and jeans, he'd filled out since I'd last seen him a few months earlier, had added a layer of muscle to his shoulders. He'd changed in other ways as well. He looked somehow focused. Substantial, where before he had seemed ephemeral. It seemed he had been spending time outdoors—his skin was tanned. He came over to me, hugged me with his free arm.

"Good to see you," he said. "You look tired. What's going on? Why the need for new locks?"

"Some kids might've been lurking around," I lied. "I had a customer with addiction problems. He worked a night shift and needed to stay awake. He wanted an herbal replacement for meth, and I think he might've been around here."

"All right," he said, his right eyebrow rising. "If you say so."

I should've known. He could always tell if I was lying. "How is your project going, by the way?" I said, changing the subject as we walked in through the back door.

He placed his toolbox on the kitchen table. "The client loves the house. I drew the designs myself."

"That's impressive." He was a self-taught renaissance man, a builder, and now an architect as well, it seemed.

He stared at me intently. "How's the husband?"

"Fine," I said quickly.

"I thought I saw him in the Starfish a couple of nights ago, sharing a cocktail with a redhead."

"Is that so? Did you say hello?" I could feel the heat in my face.

"I waved at him, but he didn't recognize me. We only met the one time."

At my mother's memorial service, when I'd cast her cremated remains into the sea. I couldn't remember Brandon and Kieran meeting, but Kieran had mentioned it later. I'd been too distraught to pay much attention.

"She's a friend," I said. "The redhead, I mean."

"Uh-huh," he said with a look of disbelief. "Okay, then. I'll start with the back door." He pulled out tools to remove the existing locks. I watched him work, shifting from foot to foot.

"Can I get you a drink? A beer?"

"I'm good," he said. "How have you been doing? It's weird coming over here without your mom around."

"I know," I said with a twinge of sadness. "Did you see her much in her last days?"

"She was getting frail. I fixed stuff for her."

"She told me she was doing better—she told me not to worry about coming back again. I'd been back and forth so much. Now I wish I'd been here—"

"Don't do that to yourself. She understood," he said.

"She died so suddenly. I thought I would have time to come back here."

"It was a surprise to me, too," he said. "She was excited about the new treatment, and then . . ."

"What?" My heart began to pound. "What new treatment?"

He wrenched out the old lock, got up, and put it on the table. Brought out a shiny new brass locking mechanism. "She didn't tell me all the details. But I thought you knew."

"No," I said, the breath thickening in my lungs. "I didn't know—I had no idea. What did she say about it? What treatment?"

"It could've bought her some time. That's all."

"How much time?" I said, as he drilled the new lock into the door, the noise grating in my ears.

"I don't know—months or years? It was a promising clinical trial . . . Wait." He stood up, rubbed his beard. "How could you not know?"

"She didn't tell me. I don't know why. Why would she tell you and not me?"

He tugged at his beard now. "Maybe she didn't want to get your hopes up."

"She still should've told me. I could've been here for her."

"Your mom was hardheaded. I thought it was sad that she died before she had a chance to start the treatment. I really thought you knew."

"No, I didn't," I said, inhaling sharply. I felt as though I'd just been hit by a bus. "That's all you know, about the treatment? I mean, maybe she ultimately decided not to go through with it. She'd already been through so much."

"No, she was going to do it. She seemed set on it."

"But there was nothing in her medical records. I got them from the clinic. Everything was in there . . ."

"There should've been notes about the trial. I don't know what to tell you."

Kieran could've been responsible for withholding pages from her records, I thought. Destroying them. He was the one who had given me her file. But that didn't make any sense. Why would he have kept the information from me? Maybe she hadn't been accepted into the experimental trial, after all. She'd died at age seventy-six, not that old in today's world, but had the researchers thought her too old? How would I know?

"I should go," I said to Brandon. "There's something I need to take care of."

"You okay? You look pale." He rested a hand on my shoulder. His dark eyes reflected my face in tiny, distorted images. He was so tall, his hand heavy.

"I'm okay," I said. "I need to make a call . . . and I might need Chantal's help with something. You're working for her, right?"

His face flushed. "Small project. I was planning to head over there later. She's home, I think. Anything I can do to help?"

"Not in this case, but thanks for offering. I need her particular expertise. Can you finish this up on your own?"

His face fell. "You call me over here so urgently, and now you're leaving?"

"Leave me an invoice," I said. "I'll catch you later."

"Yeah." He gave me a brief hug, and I was surprised at how solid he felt. I could sense that he wanted to hang on, but he reluctantly let me go. "I'll leave the front-door keys under the mat. We should talk about a surveillance system."

"Okay. I'll take a rain check." I hurried out to my car, feeling his gaze on my back. As I drove away, a flash of memory came to me, of a night months after the divorce was final. Brandon bringing over a book I'd left at the house, disappointed to see me leaving for a dinner date. He'd been freshly showered, and I'd smelled cologne. "I just got here," he'd said, "and now you're leaving? What are you wearing?"

"What?" I'd said, looking down at my little black dress.

"You shouldn't go out looking sexy."

"We're divorced, Brandon." I'd shaken my head, gotten into my car, and driven away, leaving him standing on the porch, holding the book.

Before that, he'd brought over other items I'd left behind. He'd shown up at the pharmacy just to say hello. At our wedding, his older sister, who had flown in from Wall Street only for the day, had said, before flying out again, "My brother wanted you, and he got you. When he sets his mind on something, he will never let go." But in the end, he had let me go.

Still, I felt a touch of worry. Kieran's accusation played in my head, his certainty that my ex-husband returned to the island only because of me. That was ridiculous, but had Brandon misinterpreted my request for help? No, he hadn't bothered me in a couple of years, not since my mother's death. I was sure—I hoped—he'd finally moved on.

CHAPTER EIGHT

"He's over there now?" Chantal said, standing in her open front doorway. She was in a sleek black exercise outfit.

"I left him there to finish changing the locks," I told her. "So will you help me?" I'd just told her what I wanted her to do.

"I could, but isn't it risky?" She ushered me inside and shut the door. Her house was spacious and sparsely, efficiently furnished in wood and pastels.

"If you don't want to help me, I understand," I said. "I could try different passwords and hope one of them works."

"If he's smart, you won't be able to guess his password. What if he comes by the farmhouse while we're there?"

"He's at work. He said he's got patients backed up to see him. We were supposed to go away for our anniversary. But . . ."

"You want to break into his house instead."

"Yeah, pretty much."

"Don't you have to open the shop?"

"I put a 'back later' sign on the door."

She opened the front closet and shrugged on a black coat. "What exactly are we looking for?"

"Evidence that my mother was accepted into a clinical trial before she died. And anything else I might not know about. More debts? Not that I need additional proof." I pushed aside my grief, the devastation, knowing Kieran and I should've been sharing a bottle of wine on the boat, making love in the cabin. Celebrating a year together. That my life should've been so very different.

She flipped her hair over her shoulder, buttoned up her coat. "Why would your mom's information be on his laptop?"

"I just called the clinic, and his receptionist, Mona, practically admitted to it . . . I asked her if anything might be missing from my mother's file. She said no. But she said to ask Kieran, that he had been taking work home, that he keeps files in the cloud . . ."

"She actually said that to you? Isn't it illegal for him to take patient records . . . ?"

"Kieran has been breaking a lot of rules," I said.

She motioned me to follow her into her office down the hall, uncharacteristically cluttered. I glanced at a photograph of her son and daughter on the desk. Jenny, dark haired and gorgeous, pressed her cheek to her brother's, taking a selfie. Nick was a handsome young man—he looked very much like Chantal. She followed my gaze, her eyes darkening. Then she rummaged in a drawer and produced a small USB stick. "I can boot his computer with this. It's got Linux OS on it. I can change all kinds of things, and I can even log in as an admin."

"Could you repeat that in English?" I said as we left the house.

She locked the door. "It's easy to hack into a Windows machine. If we're able to get our hands on the actual machine."

"It's there, I hope." I got into the driver's seat, started the car. "But he can't know we were there." I pulled out of the driveway.

"He won't. But this is seriously messed up. You know that, don't you?"

"Yes," I said. "If you're getting cold feet—"

"No, I'm all over this. But I do have a question." She gave me a perplexed look. "Why would he exclude the information about the trial from your mother's file?"

"I don't know." I tried not to speed down the road. On the way, I told Chantal about his debts. "He was barely making minimum payments."

"It does happen. Bill's a dentist, and he was in debt for a while. He knows doctors who owe craploads of money for their big houses, their cars, for their kids' college tuition."

"What I don't get is . . . if he wanted to make more money, Kieran could've taken a job on the mainland."

"Maybe he needed to hide away for a while," she said. "Wasn't he living in LA before? Didn't his ex-wife die? Maybe he was grieving."

She was being so charitable, defending this man who had hurt me so deeply. But maybe she was right—and Kieran was just a doctor in debt who had slipped up and slept with . . . a patient.

"When I woke up this morning, he was watching me from the doorway. He said he liked to watch me sleep."

She laughed. "That's creepy, although . . . it could be lovely under other circumstances. I wish Bill had been like that, but he wasn't romantic. He was so . . . practical."

"I'd do anything for practical right now. As long as it comes with 'loyal.'"

I floored my Honda across the island to the protected northeast coastline, where Kieran's beige farmhouse sat back from the road in the forest, the Salish Sea glinting through the trees. The restored historic structure had been his home on the island for almost five years before I'd ever met him. He'd left behind his fast-paced California life bathed in sunlight and palm trees. He'd claimed to need a change of scenery, away from memories. And he'd wanted to help Dr. Burns, who owned the clinic. She'd needed a new physician ASAP. Kieran had known her from medical school at UC Davis, where they had both studied internal medicine.

There was no sign of a car in the farmhouse driveway, but I didn't stop there. I drove past the house, around the corner, and parked on the shoulder of the road, out of view. The way Diane had parked down the road from our house, just yesterday.

Chantal and I walked back a few hundred yards to the farmhouse. I glanced up and down the road, feeling lucky that Kieran didn't have any immediate neighbors, that he owned the few acres of forest surrounding the house.

I opened the front door with his key, and we went inside. The wood floor gleamed, the walls newly painted. Kieran's deep voice played in my head, the enthusiasm in his tone when he'd told me Diane would be staging the house.

"Whoa, nice place," Chantal said.

"Yeah, he's into nice things." I felt like a stranger gazing into the living room at the soft couch and armchair, throw pillows, tables and reading lamps, a game of Scrabble on the coffee table. A memory flooded back to me, of the first time I'd set foot in here. We had dated a few times in town before he had finally invited me over for dinner. I'd spent two hours trying to choose what to wear. He'd served angel hair pasta with an exquisite wine-based sauce. The evening had been perfect, the night, too. He'd been so attentive to my needs. I couldn't bear to think of it now. My memories were marred by images of Diane here in my place. Had he wooed her the same way, with wine and romance?

"Kind of sterile, though," Chantal said, lowering her voice. It was true. There was nothing personal remaining in the room, nothing revealing. No pictures of the lovely, ethereal mother who had raised him or of his wayward father, whom she had divorced when Kieran was three. It was almost as if nobody lived here, but that was the idea of staging, to allow potential buyers to imagine the house as theirs.

"We need to find his laptop," I said. "I'm hoping he left it here. He sometimes takes it to work, but not usually. We have to be quick."

She nodded, helped me check each room on the first floor. In his office down the hall, a table, shelves, and a tilted armchair remained.

"I think that might be an Eames armchair," I said, pointing at the large office chair with a matching ottoman. "He owes a few thousand dollars on it."

She crouched to examine the chair. "There's no brand name, but I bet you're right."

His laptop computer was not in the room. "Look at this," I said. On the desk, he had printed his curriculum vitae on white cotton résumé paper.

"Is he planning to apply for a job?" she asked, peering over my shoulder. "He lists the clinic as part of his professional 'history.'"

His volunteer background included short stints in community service in Guatemala, Thailand, and Mexico. He'd worked in private practice in Covino, California. "Skill highlights," I read aloud. "'Fabulous listener,' 'heightened empathy,' and 'excellent bedside manner.' Right."

Chantal touched my shoulder. "We don't have to be here."

"No, I do need to be here. I need to know the truth." Nothing on the paper indicated his moral character, or lack thereof. "Come on, let's go upstairs."

We left the CV on the desk and ascended the wide staircase. I was aware of my breathing, every molecule alive inside me. With each step toward the master bedroom, I counted a month that I'd known him. At its threshold, my breathing grew shallow. The bed was immaculately made, but he'd dumped the suitcase and bags on the floor before rushing off to work.

"There it is," she said, rushing to his laptop, which was open on a table in the corner, the screen turned off. She sat at the desk and powered it up. The home screen prompted us for a password. The background image showed a faded photo of Kieran as a kid of maybe eight or nine, hiking with a woman on a trail in the woods. "Who's that in the picture?" she asked.

"His mother," I said. He must've scanned in the image from an old print. "But I've never seen pictures of his dad. His parents didn't come to the wedding. His mom lives down in Bandon, on the Oregon coast. We visited her there twice in her condo. She's a retired nurse. He's an only child."

Chantal looked closely. "She's like a pretty version of him."

"She once told me to accept him the way he is. Now I have a better sense of what she meant. She said he could be impulsive."

"That's an understatement."

"She adored him, though. He could do no wrong. When we were staying there, he never cleaned up or helped with the cooking or did the dishes. I helped his mom, but she never asked him to do anything. She did his laundry, hung on his every word. She adored him."

"He probably manipulated the hell out of her," Chantal said, pulling out the USB stick, plugging it into the side of the laptop.

"We mailed her a wedding invitation, but she never responded, so I called her. She said she never received it, but I know she did. I tracked the envelope. I invited her over the phone, and she said, 'Are you sure, dear?' I thought she meant, was I sure we wanted her to come to the wedding. I said, yeah, we wanted her there. But she canceled at the last minute. She said she was sick. Kieran didn't seem surprised. He came right out and said she was jealous. She barely tolerated his first marriage. But now I wonder."

"You think she was asking if you were sure you wanted to marry Kieran."

I nodded. "His dad was supposedly traveling in Europe. Kieran didn't even bother inviting him. He said his dad was an absent father who had cheated on his mom. But I was stupid. I didn't make the connection. His mom divorced his dad early in the marriage."

"Do you think she knew he was like his father?"

"Yup, probably, but she loves Kieran unconditionally, the way a mother loves her only son."

"That doesn't mean you have to love him unconditionally, too," Chantal said. She gestured to the screen. "Do you want to try a few passwords first?"

I took her place at the desk, clicked on the sign-in window, and tried a range of possible passwords, from his social security number, his July birthday, to the name of his first pet, a dog named Rambo. No luck. Nothing worked. I was locked out.

We traded places again. I hovered over her. She motioned me away. "Give the maestro a little space to work, please."

I stepped back. "How often do you do this kind of thing?"

"Oh, every day. Kidding. Pretty much never." Her fingers flew across the keyboard, various command-prompt windows popping up and disappearing, and then the desktop screen magically appeared against the background image of Kieran with his mom.

"We're in," she said. Several file folders were haphazardly arranged on the desktop.

"Wow, you're a genius." I leaned over her shoulder again. "Are you sure you don't have any qualms about doing this? Have you changed your mind?"

"Hell no. Let's see what's in here." She clicked through the tree of folders on the hard drive. "He didn't organize anything. This could take forever. You're hovering again."

I stepped back, glanced out the windows. A truck passed slowly down the road, carrying bales of hay in the back. "How long will it take to look through his files?"

"I can try certain search parameters. It won't capture everything, but it will be a start."

"Go ahead," I said, pacing, glancing out the window now and then while she typed. Occasionally, I glanced at the screen, watching windows and lists pop up.

"Okay, I'll look in the documents," she said.

"Wait." I pointed at a subfolder. "Quick look at his photos first?" I couldn't help my curiosity—and a touch of dread at what we might find.

"Your wish is my command." She opened a subfolder. "Looks like he's got his iPhone photos automatically downloading to this laptop from the cloud." She pulled up a series of photos of Kieran and me from the previous year, wedding pictures that made my stomach drop.

"Leave the wedding photos," I said. "Go back. I know he dated women here before I met him, but go back to his ex-wife. There, that folder, six years ago."

She opened the folder of photographs—clicked through several shots of cars, boats, hikes, parties, group shots. Pictures of Kieran in medical school with his colleagues, with various girlfriends. As a child with his mother in California, then in Oregon. "No pictures of Dad," Chantal said. "Wait, there's one."

"He looks exactly like his father," I said, peering closely at the man in the suit, CEO of a hybrid-aircraft company. "Not much in those eyes."

"Can you even tell?" Chantal said. "He looks like a nice man to me." She clicked through to other photos.

"Wait, there, that must be his ex-wife," I said, my pulse quickening. I glanced out the window. The road was empty. I looked back at the screen. "I've never seen any pictures of her."

The first one showed Kieran and a young, slim woman at a distance on a beach. "Looks like a nice climate. Palm trees," Chantal said. She clicked to the next one, a closer view of Kieran on his yacht with the same woman, her hair tied back tightly in a ponytail.

"She was beautiful," I said.

"Botox and breast implants." Chantal flipped her hair back over her shoulder. She clicked through a few more shots of Kieran and his wife in various luxurious locations, in various glamorous poses. He was dressed in pastel colors, deeply tanned and fit.

"He's got gel in his hair," I said. "It's like he's a different person."

"He's a chameleon," Chantal said.

"Wait, stop there. The one before that."

She clicked back to an image of Kieran and his wife standing in a group in front of an immense Italian villa, against the backdrop of the Santa Ynez Mountains. "Zoom in," I said. "On the faces."

"Looks like her family," she said, zooming in on various people. "That must be their home or something. Looks like he married into money."

"But he's so much in debt."

"He burned his way through the cash, maybe, if he ever got his hands on it."

"His wife looks thin. She didn't look that skinny in some of the others. Go back again."

Chantal kept clicking back. "How much time do you want to spend on this woman? There are other folders."

"Just a bit longer. There's something . . . She's thinner in each picture, maybe?"

"Hard to tell. Maybe she was on a diet."

"She died of the flu, he told me."

Chantal sat back and looked at me. "Is there any way you can know for sure?"

"I'm not family—I couldn't possibly get any medical information about her."

"What about a Google search?" Her fingers were already flying, and an online obituary popped up for Kieran's wife.

"She was only thirty when she died," I said. "A year before he moved to the island—seven years ago. She would've been thirty-eight now. He's forty."

"Née Lana Ellison," Chantal read. "She was heir to her family's fortune, made from brands of applesauce and condiments. They were philanthropists. She loved to play tennis and volunteer for local charities.

This doesn't tell us much." She pulled up a local newspaper article about Lana, in which her distraught mother urged everyone to get their flu shots. Lana had apparently contracted the flu, her fever had spiked, and Kieran had found her unconscious on the bathroom floor and rushed her to the ER, where she died an hour later.

"How terrible," I said. "We should hurry now. Let's look for—"

"Anything with your mother's name on it. Medical records? You're hovering again. I can do this fast if you're not looking over my shoulder all the time."

"Sorry, thank you," I said, going into the bathroom. I could hear her tapping away on the keyboard. Kieran's shaving brush and razor sat on the tile countertop next to the sink, and I could smell the peppermint soap he loved. *Funny,* I thought, *the way we know certain intimate things about people we love, or have loved, and yet maybe we never know them at all.*

"Here we go." She motioned me back into the room. "These are downloaded files, letters, not records." She opened the first letter from a research center on the East Coast, dated only a couple of weeks before my mother's death.

"She was accepted into the experimental trial," I said. "Brandon was right. The treatment involved injecting modified immune cells into the tumor . . . It could have halted the growth of her tumors for several months, or even years."

"Here's another letter," she said, clicking to open another file. "This one gives her instructions for arriving at the research center and outlines some of the preliminary tests she would have to undergo. Looks like she was on track to enter the trial."

I sat on the bed, my legs weak, my arms heavy at my sides. A cold wind blew through me. "Why didn't he tell me? Do you think she even saw the letters?"

"Probably not." Chantal glanced out the window, then back at the screen. "I'll copy those documents to the USB drive, and then we should get going. I'm nervous."

"Me, too," I said, twisting my hands in my lap. "Thank you for doing this."

She tapped away, while I sat with my head in my hands. She stopped, staring at the screen.

"What is it?" I said, jumping up to look over her shoulder. She was opening and closing windows at lightning speed.

"He didn't clear the cache on his browser," she said. "He was looking at luxury property listings from a high-end real estate firm in Seattle. He made these pages his favorites."

"He can't afford these homes," I said. *Unless he were to inherit my estate.* I began to feel sick to my stomach again.

"He likes expensive houses. Not a crime, but . . . surprising." She had a peculiar look on her face.

"Did he look up anything else? Like methods of murder? How to dispose of a body?" I laughed nervously.

"I don't know what he searched for before the real estate. He cleared his browsing history."

As if he had something to hide, I thought, nausea rising inside me. As she shut down the computer, the bile rose in my throat, and I barely made it to the bathroom before I threw up into the toilet.

CHAPTER NINE

Chantal stood on her porch and waved goodbye to Elise. The poor thing was fighting the flu, or maybe just sick from the loss of her hopes, her shattered illusions. Nothing to be done. Chantal had tried to help. They had gleaned so much from Kieran's computer, and from the files and photographs he had so casually left on his hard drive in a flotsam of disorganization.

After Elise's car disappeared around the bend, Chantal went around to the backyard, carried two pots of blooming black-eyed Susans to her Kia, and put them into the back seat. *Rudbeckia fulgida*, Selene had called them. Elise's mother had known the scientific names for just about every flower under the sun.

Then Chantal wrote a note to Jenny and drove the flowers to the graveyard, planted them around Jenny's headstone. She wiped the granite clean. Below the name, Jennifer Gittner, and her birth and death dates, the epitaph read, JUST WHISPER MY NAME IN YOUR HEART, AND I WILL BE THERE.

But Jenny had not come to Chantal, as often and fervently as she had whispered her daughter's name. The stones in the cemetery were a cruel joke. They did not mark where a spirit could be found. Jenny was everywhere. She was in the sea, in the clouds, in the leaves, in the squirrels scampering through the garden. She was in Chantal's memory, coming to the surface at any slight trigger—the sight of a baby in a stroller, conjuring the time Jenny had dropped her Binky down the storm drain on Waterfront Road.

Whenever Chantal passed a neighbor's garden full of fluffy, free-roaming hens, she remembered the time when Jenny, at eight or nine, had hugged a hen named Hannah, said, "I love chickens"—and never eaten meat again. How could such a compassionate light ever be extinguished?

Jenny would be born again in another form—her love could not die. So many times, Chantal had seen signs in the flap of a hawk's wing, in the hovering iridescent hummingbirds at the fuchsia plants.

Chantal placed her folded note beneath a rock on the grave, another reply to the note her daughter had left behind, when she had expressed her despair. She had written a list of items with instructions about who would get what. The decision to walk into the ocean had given her relief. *Nothing was ever clearer to me. I'm at peace.*

Neither Chantal nor Bill had understood the depth of her sadness, although they had sensed her depression. She hadn't been eating much, had been rude and sullen. The psychotherapist had diagnosed reactive depression. But they never knew what she'd been reacting to, and she had missed her last two appointments.

Nick, two years older, had been clueless, already planning his departure to Korea. He had always dreamed of traveling. Chantal missed him with a sharp pain—Skyping was never enough, but it was better than nothing. She understood why he didn't want to come back to the memories.

Chantal, on the other hand, lived inside them. She often tried to understand what it must've been like for Jenny to slip into unconsciousness as she sank into the cold water. She had imagined wading in to be with her daughter. So many times, she had played back the events of that morning. She should have woken earlier. Should have checked Jenny's room. Should have gone looking for her.

Chantal sat for a time on the bench next to the grave, feeling the rain in her hair, dampening her face, her clothes. She talked to Jenny, and then she walked down the path to Mike's grave. Her first husband's headstone was off by itself, covered in moss, weeds growing up over the plot. He was Jenny's biological father, but Jenny didn't remember much about him. He'd died when she was only three years old. But Nick had been five. He remembered—and he was far away now.

Chantal had not buried Jenny near Mike. She rarely came this far into the cemetery. Strangely, the closer she got to him, the tighter her muscles became, the less she could breathe. There was another bench here, older, well-worn wood. "You're the reason for everything I do now," she said to him. "Even though you are dead. You were too young, I know." She sat on the bench, talking to him as she often did. He knew, for example, that she had moved away from the island with the kids, soon after his death. She had learned computer programming on the mainland, had started again, away from memories. He knew she had met Bill, had married him. He knew that Bill had been a loving stepfather to Jenny and Nick. He knew that she and Bill had moved back to the island for the slower pace, when Jenny got depressed and started missing school. They'd thought she would be happier here. "I did my best," Chantal told Mike. "But it wasn't enough. And now there is all of this going on. And I need to do something about it." She sat there, telling a dead man the details of her plans.

CHAPTER TEN

I stood beneath the stark bathroom bulb, staring at the telltale blue lines on the pregnancy test stick. I felt myself tumbling headlong into an abyss. Now what? *Now what?* This couldn't be happening—the timing couldn't have been worse. It was the universe laughing at me, showing me again that I was never in control.

After I'd dropped Chantal at home, I'd raced down to the pharmacy to buy the set of two pregnancy tests. I hadn't recognized the clerk behind the counter, but she had smiled at me and said, "Hello, Mrs. Lund." *Damn it,* I'd thought. I'd looked up to see Lily Kim, owner of the shop, waving at me from behind the pharmacy counter. She had offered me a job when I'd first returned to the island, but I had declined, knowing she didn't need another pharmacist and probably couldn't afford to hire one. But she had loved my mother. I'd been grateful for her gesture of goodwill, but this time, I hadn't stayed around to chat. I'd run out of the store, hoping Lily Kim and her employee would not gossip about what I had bought.

When I'd arrived home, Brandon had finished installing the locks and had left the keys under the mat. I'd run upstairs, torn open the tests. Each one yielded a positive result. I didn't have room for this, for the confirmation of what I had feared when I'd vomited into the toilet at Kieran's farmhouse. I gripped the handle of the second plastic stick between my forefinger and thumb, staring at it, my body tense. I should have known. I should have suspected. The irritability, nausea.

The calendar should have given me a clue, too, the number of weeks that had passed since my last period—nearly seven. But sometimes I skipped periods. It was not unusual. My rhythm had always been erratic, and Brandon and I had tried so hard, for so long, never succeeding, that somehow I'd thought I could never conceive.

But, of course, that had been a false assumption, since Brandon had been the source of our problem. Now here was the proof, the result I'd always hoped for—yet I dreaded having to tell Kieran I was pregnant. Maybe I never would. But the baby was his. He would be forever tied to his offspring, to me. Would the child turn out like him? A liar or worse? I had no idea.

I threw the pregnancy test stick into the garbage with the other one. No matter what, now I had another life inside me to protect. Everything of mine would become my child's. Everything was different now. The child would need me, would need a safe and happy life.

My mind raced ahead. I needed to buy baby clothes, convert the guest room into a nursery. Add this to my conversation with my attorney when he called me back. Call my ob-gyn in the city, Dr. Gupta, make an appointment. Schedule an ultrasound, blood tests. Take prenatal vitamins. Stop drinking caffeine—when had I last had a cup of coffee? I'd drunk herbal tea that morning. When had I last taken any kind of over-the-counter medication? I couldn't remember. I hadn't drunk any alcohol—no whisky or wine—not recently, anyway, but I'd inhaled Diane's cigarette smoke, which now enraged me. *How dare she?* I wanted her to disappear from the face of the earth. She had contaminated my house, my lungs, my baby. I had been pregnant when I'd come home from the city—and before I'd left. For a few weeks now.

In my childhood bed, I crossed my arms over my abdomen, curled up in the fetal position. Kieran had a right to know, but he would use the baby as an excuse to cajole his way back into the house—for what purpose? Did he love me, or did he simply want my money?

If only none of this had happened. In my original conception of him, he would've been a great father. His young patients loved him. He made them feel at ease. He was playful, fun. But now I knew he was disloyal and possibly worse. He could threaten me and my baby. After what we'd found in his computer, the worst possibilities coalesced in my mind. Kieran had possibly hastened my mother's death by preventing her from entering the experimental trial. What else to make of those letters? And why had he done it? It had to be money. Triggering my inheritance. Then there would be only my death to wait for—or hasten. *The long game.*

Give me the answers, I thought to my mother. *How do I get through this? Did you plan to enter that clinical trial? Or did Kieran stop you? Did he lie to you?*

I got up, went downstairs to make a sandwich, but I barely tasted what I was eating. Outside the kitchen window, a pileated woodpecker hammered away at a dead fir snag, poking holes in the bark, its red crest brilliant in the light. The bird was a female. Her forehead was black. The male has a red forehead, Kieran had told me. The binoculars he'd given me sat on the windowsill—it was so difficult to believe that we had done something as innocuous as watch birds together, that I had believed nothing bad could happen between us.

As the light faded into evening, I went upstairs to change into pajamas. When in doubt, try to sleep, my mother had told me when I was young. Everything is always clearer in the morning. And I knew Kieran could not get into the house since I'd changed the locks. I had not told him.

It took me a while to fall asleep, my mind spinning—*I need to protect myself, my baby.* I was unsure when, but I fell asleep and woke outside in the front garden, still in my pajamas, shivering. A strip of orange lit the eastern horizon.

I spun around, breathing fast. What was I doing out here? I could smell the leaves, feel the cold, wet ground squishing between my bare toes. I hadn't put on my slippers. My teeth chattered. The silhouettes of bushes and trees brushed against the sky. I couldn't remember descending the stairs, walking outside. The previous morning, I'd slid my feet into my slippers. They'd been damp, but I hadn't paid attention. And Kieran said he'd seen me coming back from the cottage early in the morning, before I'd left for the city. I'd done it again. Walked in my sleep.

I could hear a voice, the bang of a door. Someone was calling for me. Brandon.

"What's going on? Elise, are you okay?" He ran up to me from the driveway, dressed in his bulky canvas work pants and jacket.

"I was just . . . checking the garden. I thought I heard something. What are you doing here?"

"Getting an early start on the deck before I head to the construction site."

"No, here, at my house. What are you doing here?" My voice came out raspy, and I tried to clear the cobwebs from my brain.

"I was headed this way anyway. I came to check on you. It's a big deal, changing the locks. I was worried about you."

"I'm fine, thank you," I said absentmindedly.

"You were sleepwalking again, weren't you?"

"No," I said quickly. "I meant to be outside."

"Barefoot?" He frowned.

"I was in a hurry . . . I heard a noise."

I followed his gaze toward the cottage. The lights were on, the door slightly ajar. I rushed inside, and he followed. I tried to remember coming out here. The front room was a mess, as if I'd tried to rearrange the displays in my sleep, with no sense of logic.

"You heard something out here?" Brandon said. "Should I call the cops? Was this a break-in?" He whipped his cell phone out of his pocket.

72

"No, don't call anyone," I said, heading into the prep room. "I think it was me. I came out here in my sleep."

"Shit, Elise. Not again. What if you'd gotten lost or walked all the way to the ocean?"

"I wouldn't do that," I said.

"How do you know?"

The truth was, I didn't. "I guess I'm under stress," I said.

"Chantal mentioned you and your husband—"

"We're fine. Don't go there, please." Behind the counter, in the prep room, my mother's row of cloth journals had tipped over again like dominoes.

The weigh scale sat on the table, a dusting of powder on top. Right behind the scale, a bag labeled SLUMBER had fallen off the shelf. I returned the bag to the shelf.

"You're not fine," he said, coming up to rest his hands on my shoulders. "I'm worried about you. Remember what happened back at our old place?"

"Yes, of course I do." I slipped away from him, grabbed a roll of paper towels, and started wiping the countertop clean.

"You were out in the backyard," he said, coming up behind me. "What if I hadn't found you?"

"I would've woken up on my own."

"Yeah, sometime after you'd gone out through the gate and wandered off."

I'd come to my senses staring at the latch on the cedar-fence gate behind the Craftsman-style home we had so carefully remodeled in Seattle. "But I didn't."

"You could have. What about the time before that? When I caught you with the scissors?"

I clenched the paper towel, remembering how I'd woken to find I was holding a pair of sharp scissors in one hand and a piece of paper in the other. I'd looked at the gleaming blades in shock, gasped, and dropped the scissors on the desk. I'd been cutting up the medical report that I had discovered in his pocket the day before. I'd confronted him. We'd argued, gone to bed furious with each other. Before I slept, I'd made the decision to leave him.

He'd grown the beginning of a beard overnight. I'd forgotten how quickly his hair could grow. I'd called him my mountain man, also because of his height, six foot six, but he hadn't been brawny back then. He'd stared at the strips of paper on his desk, his mouth open, and I'd jumped to my feet, nearly knocking over his office chair. I'd looked at my hands, somehow expecting to see them bloody and cut to pieces, too, but I was okay. He hadn't yelled at me, hadn't called me crazy. Instead, he had helped me gather up the strips of paper. "You need me," he'd said gently. "I can take care of you when this happens. We can't split up, don't you see?"

Soon after that incident, I'd filed for divorce. We had already been falling apart, piece by piece. His lie had been the final straw. "I'm stressed, that's all," I'd said. But in the back of my mind, I'd worried about what I might be capable of doing in my sleep.

Now here I was, and here he was again, witnessing my craziness. "You need someone to watch over you," he said gently. "Where is your husband now?" He glanced back in the direction of the house.

"He's not here," I said, and maybe he could tell, by the look on my face, that he shouldn't ask any more questions.

"I'll help you clean up then," he said.

"You don't need to—"

"I have a few minutes."

As I rearranged the displays, Brandon swept the floor, and it was almost as though we were a couple again—the synergy between us fell back into place. But I knew it was an illusion, that the cooperation inevitably turned sour.

In the prep room, he propped the broom against the wall and crouched down, reaching beneath a cabinet of drawers. I lost sight of him, and then he pulled out something rectangular and flat, a cloth-bound journal, weathered and worn, the painted pattern on the cover a decoupage garden of lilies and leaves and butterflies.

"Look what I found," he said, coming to me. "Is this yours?"

"No," I said. "It was under the cabinet?"

"Must've fallen from up there," he said, nodding toward the journals on the shelf.

"It must be my mother's." I took the journal from him, opened the front cover. The cursive inside was familiar and unmistakable. It was my mother's journal, and by the dates she had scrawled inside, I could tell it was her most recent one, the last journal in which she had written before her death. But it was different from the others. On the first page she had written, perhaps as a note to herself: *Keep hidden.*

CHAPTER ELEVEN

I rushed Brandon off, making a quick excuse. After he drove away, I took the diary into the main house, straight into the large library, and sat at my mother's desk, the mottled light filtering in, the garden in motion outside. She had spent many days sitting here, paying bills or poring over the reference books that packed her shelves. I imagined her writing in this delicate cloth journal.

Her words still breathed, her elegant handwriting dancing across the page. Why had she wanted this book hidden? Inside, she had drawn intricate pictures of common herbs—white willow bark, capsaicin, calendula. She had drawn feverfew, had noted below the picture, *For migraines.* And beneath a sketch of lemon balm, she had written *curly-edged, mintlike leaves a staple ingredient in my facials and tinctures.*

She had also sketched castor beans, the deadliest poison on Earth if the ricin is not extracted. A single bean could kill an adult within five minutes. My mother had used the seeds without the hull for medicinal tinctures.

Her writings became gradually sparser, more disjointed, blank pages between entries.

The spider weaves a speedy web, or should I call it an octopus-like alien, its tentacles reaching through my brain.

I swallowed, the room closing in. She was writing about her tumor. More blank pages, then:

The headaches plague me. When I awaken, my body aches. My fingers are stiff. Soon, I won't be able to write much. The words drop from my mind and wither away.

She had put on such a brave face when I'd visited. Had told me not to worry.

Elise feels so hopeless after the divorce. I can't bear to tell her that her Brandon has been here, fixing the faulty light switches, the door hinges, the plumbing leak beneath the kitchen sink. Talking to him is a comfort. I can't burden her. But I have decisions to make.

What decisions? About her estate? Her treatment? About my ex-husband?

Dr. Lund is attentive and knowledgeable.

An entry about Kieran, but then nothing more about him as she wrote on about difficult customers who demanded easy solutions or wanted deep discounts for remedies. More blank pages.
And then:

Dr. L is dating Elise. I only hope his intentions are good. He seems like a man who keeps secrets.

She didn't know how right she had been.
Another blank page, and then:

Shouldn't have told Dr. Lund about the Juliet, should not have confessed . . .

What had she meant? Confessed to what? I couldn't make sense of her words. Her handwriting had devolved over time, her writing messier, choppy in her last days, her thoughts breaking apart.

On the second-to-last page, below an illegible entry, my mother had written:

I must warn Elise about Dr. L . . .

I nearly dropped the journal. My hands shook. My throat went dry. The library seemed to whisper behind my back, the books conspiring against me. Another blank page, and then:

If I die now, it was not an accident. It was Dr. L. He will use the Juliet.

I read the phrases again and again. She must have been delusional. The tumor must have taken control of her brain, making her paranoid.

Dr. L could have been another doctor. No, she had meant Kieran. Dr. Lund.

I thought she had still been in possession of her faculties when I'd spoken to her on the phone, and she had told me not to worry. But her messy writing suggested all reason had begun to leave her.

If I die now, it was not an accident.
It was Dr. L.

I flipped back through her notes. Some earlier entries bled into a blur. The letters faded at their edges. My mother had suffered from headaches, difficulty writing—that much was clear. Difficulty thinking straight. I'd begun to detect subtle changes over the phone, in her periods of silence, her quick shift from one subject to another, but I had dismissed the signs. Occasional listlessness, bouts of anger. I'd been in denial, not wanting to believe my mother was dying.

I had already accompanied her to surgery, chemo, radiation treatments. She'd been so exhausted afterward. I'd deluded myself into believing she could be cured, but even then, I'd known that wasn't possible. She had been buying precious time, that was all. How much more time would she have had if she had started the clinical trial?

The journal must've been on the shelf with the other ones, hiding in plain sight. I had flipped through a couple of the journals, but my grief had been too raw. I still dropped into a chasm of sorrow when I saw her handwriting, but I should've paid more attention.

I never expected her to accuse anyone of murder, least of all her doctor. When she had crumpled in the garden, suffering from a stroke, he had signed off on her death certificate—but what if she had not died of a stroke at all?

A shiver ran through me, my eyes watering. A breeze rustled through the trees, disturbing the plants on the library windowsill. The leaves of the devil's ivy fluttered—they were almost impossible to kill. Unlike fragile human beings. Unlike my mother.

He will use the Juliet.

The Juliet could kill, she said. She warned me not to touch it, said it had already killed someone. But whom? Had she told Kieran that she knew the herb could kill? Maybe she'd had the idea in her mind that he might kill her somehow, and her focus on the Juliet plant had been the delusional part of her thinking. If he'd planned to kill her, why wouldn't he have used an established drug? He was a doctor. He had any manner of pharmaceuticals at his disposal.

I looped back to the possibility that she had been delusional. But if not, I couldn't prove that he had wanted to kill her or, in the extreme case, that he had done so. I did not even have her cremated remains.

But the prospect that she might have met with foul play made me hyperventilate. Kieran had made house calls to check on her, even after she'd started seeing her oncologist for treatments in the city. He could have opened her mail. Perhaps he had grown impatient waiting for her to die, and he'd sped up the process.

No, never. What horrible thoughts. How could he have been sure that I would marry him? Arrogance? An overblown sense of his own abilities and importance? He did get what he wanted, almost always, it seemed. In the event of my death, he would inherit all of my assets, including the house and gardens, which I owned outright.

If Kieran wanted to kill me, he would try to make it look natural. Or like an accident—but no, what was I even thinking? I had only a few words in my mother's journal about a plant in the garden and her irrational fear that Kieran wanted to kill her with it.

I flipped through the pages again. She had tucked a folded, fragile slip of paper into the back pocket of the journal. It was a page from an earlier journal, with the notation *Book #12* in the top-right corner. Her writing, in black marker, had bled in a few places. She had drawn a picture of an herb with jagged leaves and narrow stems resembling lovage, but with the spindly look of chervil, similar to cilantro. She labeled the herb *Juliet*. It was a beautiful likeness of the herb in the garden.

She had written *Slumber* and, below the word, several recipes with notes. So the Slumber powder had contained the Juliet. I'd read her formulas before, so I understood the meanings of the words: *marc*, which referred to the solid matter in the formula; *menstruum*, or liquid, in this case alcohol and water; and *precipitate*, the residue that settled to the bottom. The recipes changed, some numbers crossed out, ingredients added or subtracted. Sometimes she included lavender, chamomile, or licorice, hibiscus, passionflower.

Formulas for Slumber, including the crushed Juliet plant. At the bottom of the page, she had scrawled the name C. Farrell, and then her writing appeared to have continued on another page.

I went to the cottage to look through the cloth journals on the shelf, numbered on their spines, and pulled down Book #12. Flipped through the brittle pages. This journal was dated nearly seventeen years earlier, after I'd left for college. The book was fragile, coming apart at the spine, but I found the jagged edge of the missing page. On the page that came after, on the line following the words *C. Farrell*, she had written "one bottle" for "one-time use." And then:

First time, not enough. Adjust dosage. Pandora's box in the wrong dose... deceptive... like Romeo and Juliet. Untraceable.

Romeo and Juliet? What had she meant? *Untraceable.* Did this mean the plant was not traceable in the human system, and how would she know? She had traveled to gardens around the world, had smuggled cuttings and seeds back in her luggage. Sometimes she didn't know exactly what she had brought home.

I knew this much—that my husband needed my money, that he had cheated on me. That he had lied. That my mother had feared him, that she had thought he would use the Juliet plant to kill her. That he and Diane had spoken cryptically, in a way that I could easily interpret as a plan to kill me as well.

I looked at my mother smiling at me from her photograph, but now she seemed sad, or worried, her gaze imploring me to do something, but what?

My attorney had not yet called back. I wished he would hurry. Maybe it was time to go into town to talk to the police. I had known a local deputy, John Russell, in high school. These days, I said hello when I saw him in town or on patrol. He had known my mother, had attended her funeral. I zipped the journal in my purse, locked up the house and cottage, and floored the Honda all the way down to the precinct.

CHAPTER TWELVE

The police station was in a bungalow with a metal roof, the words SAN JUAN COUNTY SHERIFF, CHINOOK ISLAND STATION printed on the side of the building. An American flag flapped on a tall metal pole by the front door. Two dark-green patrol cars, with the block letters SHERIFF painted on the back, were parked in the lot.

I pulled into a visitor spot and went inside, jumpy and nervous. Did I really want to involve the police? John Russell and I had known each other a long time ago, before he'd left for the police academy and then to work patrol on the streets of Reno. He'd returned to the island a few years earlier, or so my mother had told me. How well did he remember me?

In the reception area, there was nobody behind the desk, but I heard laughter in a back room. I rang the bell at the counter, and the laughter ceased. The smell of pine cleanser hung in the air. I waited, my heartbeat fast. A uniformed officer came out, pulling up his belt, and grinned at me. I'd never seen him before.

"Help you, ma'am?" He was tall, his name tag reading OFFICER WILEY.

"I'm here to talk to Deputy Russell," I said in a shaky voice. "Does he still work here?"

"He still does," John Russell said, coming up behind the other officer.

Officer Wiley nodded at me and headed out the front door.

John's bushy brows rose. "Elise, good to see you!" Since I'd run into him a few months earlier, he'd put on a few pounds. He wore a button-down blue shirt, open at the top, a stain on the front, a clip-on tie clinging to one side of his collar. I smiled at him, at his gray, concerned eyes, the prominent nose with a bump in the middle.

"I need to talk to you off the record, if possible," I said as he shook my hand. His fingers felt slightly sticky.

He ushered me into a conference room that smelled of stale coffee. A watercooler, fridge, and counter took up one wall, a dry-erase board on the opposite wall. A tinted bay window overlooked the front garden and the sidewalk. He pulled out a chair for me.

"Coffee, tea? We might have soda—"

"I'm good, thanks," I said, sitting at the table. He poured himself a cup of coffee from a pot on a burner and sat across from me. I noticed two stains on his shirt.

"How can I help you?" he said. "You look . . . worried."

"It has been a bad couple of days." I wiped my cheeks, aware suddenly of how unkempt I must look. "I imagine you're busy. I won't take much of your time."

"We've got four deputies now, so my stress level is easing up. I get exciting calls, though. Just checked on a dog that was supposedly hit by a car. Turned out he was fine, sunning himself in the driveway. What's going on with you?"

I couldn't help but smile a little. "I need some advice about my husband."

"Dr. Lund? Is he okay?"

"I'm not sure. I think he might be trying to . . ." I lowered my voice, glanced toward the open doorway. I looked back at John. "He's having

83

an affair. I caught them together. And it turns out he has a lot of debt. But that's not why I'm here."

"Whoa, I'm sorry, Elise," John said, gulping his coffee.

I took the journal out of my purse and slid it across the table. "And then there's this. My mother's journal. Her last one before she died."

"Should I be writing up a report?" John said, sitting back, lifting his hands in the air. "The minute I look at this, I'll need to file a report."

"You can't just . . . talk to me?"

He slid the journal back toward me. "Go ahead and tell me what's on your mind."

I tucked the journal back into my purse. "She says her doctor would be the one to kill her, if she were to die 'now.' She wrote 'now,' meaning before her time. I found evidence in Kieran's laptop that she was accepted into a clinical trial that might have extended her life, but she never entered the trial. And he didn't even mention that she was going to try."

John frowned, ran the flat of his hand up over his forehead. "Have you spoken to him about this? Asked him about the trial?"

"He would deny everything. I just think he might've done something to her. To my mother. But I don't know."

"Your mom—didn't she have a stroke? She also had cancer. I knew that."

"Yes," I said, growing more frustrated, "but . . ."

He leaned forward, clasped his hands on the table. "Are you saying you think your husband, her doctor, might have killed her?"

"No, I don't know—I think this all might've been his plan to marry me for my money," I said, realizing how crazy I sounded.

His frown deepened, a furrow appearing on his forehead. "Do you have any proof of this? How do you know?"

"I overheard him talking to his lover, and it seemed like they were talking about getting rid of me. She said she wanted me gone already, and he told her to be patient and to learn to play the long game."

John let out a low whistle, took another gulp of coffee. "Did you hear them say anything more specific?" He whipped a notepad from his shirt pocket and laid it on the table, fished out a pen and jotted notes.

"Just those words. She said she wanted it to be 'done' and she wanted me 'gone already,' and Kieran said to be 'patient, chill out' and something about how she should learn to play the long game."

John kept shaking his head, dropped the pen on the pad of paper. "All this just happened?"

"Yes, two days ago," I said, shaking now. "I asked Kieran about it, but he put me off."

John sat back, ran his hand down his face. "Do you have any evidence that they might be planning to harm you?"

"You mean aside from what I heard and read?"

"You don't have a recording, a phone message? Evidence of a specific plan?"

"No," I said faintly.

He whipped a crumpled tissue from his pocket and blew his nose. "How long did you know him before you married him?" He downed the rest of his coffee.

I focused on a robin alighting on the alder tree outside the window. "I've known him only three years. We dated for a while, then I broke things off. But he actually wanted to marry me after six months." I remembered now, Kieran kissing the palm of my hand, all the way up my arm, saying, "Why not get married right now? We can go to the courthouse . . ."

"You refused him?"

"It was too soon," I said, thinking back, understanding now that Kieran had been rushing things. "And then my mom got sick. I wonder if he knew . . ."

"That she was sick?"

"That she was dying. I moved back to the mainland, but I was coming back here to take her to doctors' appointments and treatments.

I wasn't seeing him for a while. But when she died, he was there . . . for me."

"And you married him after how long?"

"Six months later," I said. "We've been married a year. It was too fast."

John shrugged, picked up the pen again, rolled it between his fore-finger and thumb. "People get married after three weeks. You never know. Did he take out a large life insurance policy on you?"

My shoulders tensed. "No, not that I know of."

"Do you have one on him?"

"What? No!"

"How much does he stand to inherit in the event of your death?"

"Nearly five million dollars," I said, and I could feel my lips trembling.

"Whoa." John dropped the pen on the notepad again, picked it up. "That's quite a chunk of cash."

"I've got a call in to my attorney to change my will. Sometimes he takes a day or two to check his messages."

"All right," John said carefully. "Has your husband shown any other signs that he wants your money, other than his debts?"

I sighed. "No—he likes fast cars, expensive gifts."

"Don't we all."

I could feel the blood rushing to my face. "Well, I don't."

He slicked back his hair. "Liking expensive things is not a crime I could investigate. Or overheard conversations. Has he posted anything on social media?"

"Not that I know of," I said. "But I didn't check. He told me he doesn't have social media accounts."

"Anything in any emails?"

"I didn't read them. I don't have his passwords."

"Any phone calls or other indications? Rumors?"

My blood thickened, slowing in my veins. "Not that I know of."

"You share a computer?"

"No, no. He's got his own."

"Texts on his cell phone?"

"I don't know his code, no." I frowned.

"The journal in your purse, what did your mother write in it?"

"She was afraid he might kill her. This was a few weeks before she died. But . . ."

"Your mother was suffering from a brain tumor," John said, sitting back. "I don't know if you realize this, but I was once called to pick her up. She was wandering the street in her nightgown. I took her home. She begged me not to tell anyone."

"What?" My insides turned to mush. "Who called you?"

"A passing motorist—they were concerned about her out on the main road. Luckily she didn't get far from your house."

"You should have called me!"

He opened his arms. "Hey, she didn't want me to. She seemed lucid to me. I took her to the clinic. Dr. Lund saw her. Turned out she was sleepwalking. Apparently she had done that before. She didn't want us to call anyone, and there was no reason to."

"But there was," I said, my voice breaking. "She was my mother."

"I know you loved her, Elise, but she was a grown-up. I thought she was confused, but I had to honor her wishes."

"You thought she was confused. You mean, what she wrote in the journal—you think she was delusional."

He tapped the pen on the table. "It's a possibility. It crossed your mind, too, didn't it? Dr. Lund is a well-respected physician. People love him. Your mother was very ill, Elise. Let's say he did want to do away with her, or planned to . . . What could I do about it now? We don't have a body or any other proof. Nothing. She was cremated."

I got up, shaking, my legs almost buckling. "You know what? You're right. It was a mistake to come here."

"Whoa, wait a second." John got up, too, motioned me to sit down again, but I didn't. We were both standing there on opposite sides of the table. John rubbed his upper lip. "Look, if you want me to write up a report, I will."

"No, why should you? You can't do anything for me."

"All right, for now, I'll kiss off the paperwork."

"You think I'm jumping to conclusions—maybe I am."

He ran his hand down his face, touched the clip-on tie dangling from his collar. "I didn't say that, exactly."

"But you meant it."

"It's a terrible thing, your spouse cheating on you. Your mom passing away . . . and with what she wrote, nobody could blame you for jumping to conclusions."

"What about what Kieran and his lover were saying?"

"You know, maybe they were just talking. Lovers talk. They exaggerate."

"Right," I said, the walls closing in. I needed to get out of there.

"If something more specific happens, come on in and talk to me and I'll write it up. Unless you want me to have a talk with your husband. I could do that. If you want. Go down and have a chat with him."

"And ask him what? If he's planning to kill me for my money?" I laughed, shaking my head.

"Yeah," he said. "That's exactly what I mean."

"No!" I shouted, holding up my hand. "He would only get angry. I'd be in worse danger. You think I'm being ridiculous, and I see it now. I am. I'm losing it—I don't know what came over me. Please don't talk to him."

"Yeah, okay, you got it. But I thought I'd offer." He followed me to the front door. "Nothing I can do if no crime has been committed. I walk a fine line. But when you've got something more, come in and—"

"You'll write up a report. Thank you," I said.

He handed me his business card. "Call me anytime, Elise, and take care."

CHAPTER THIRTEEN

Take care—right. What was I supposed to do to take care of myself? I fumed all the way home. Locked the journal in a drawer in the cottage, beneath a stack of papers. In the main house, I paced the rooms. It wasn't long before I heard the rumble of Kieran's car racing up the driveway. My heart rate kicked up immediately. What was he doing here, yet again? The guy never gave up. *It's what you do when you're after five million dollars,* I thought in a panic. But he couldn't get in, thank goodness. I was so glad Brandon had changed the locks.

A minute later, I heard his key in the front door, and then he was ringing the doorbell, over and over. My veins froze. *Just breathe. Keep calm.* I went to the front door, but I didn't open it. "What do you want?"

"You changed the fucking locks!" he yelled. "You can't do that."

"I can! Go away!" I yelled through the door, the words in my mother's journal spinning around and around in my head. *Must warn Elise.*

There was silence, then the sound of scuffling and branches scraping the house, and then he pressed his nose to the picture window in the living room. "Open the door. We need to talk."

A cold dread rippled across my skin. *I shouldn't feel this way about my own husband,* I thought. Then I admonished myself, tried to convince

myself that my mother had become paranoid. *He's the man you knew—
not loyal, but normal in other ways.* Or was he?

"We'll talk through my attorney!" I said.

A look of fear, then disbelief, crossed his face. "Come on—we
haven't even sat down together to work through this! Why do we need
an attorney?" His voice was muffled through the window, the privet
bush snagging on his jacket. For once, I wished the house were not
so secluded, out of earshot of helpful neighbors. "I miss you," he said,
pressing the flat of his hand to the window. "Come on. We need to
talk."

"Give me time," I said. "I need to think! I have to open the shop
today. I've been closed for a week. Go away."

Abruptly, he disappeared from view. I dashed through the foyer,
peered out through the dining room window, hoping he'd gone back
to his car, which I could see parked at an angle in the driveway. But the
car stayed where it was. *The back door.*

I turned and raced down the hall, moving in slow motion, as if
through quicksand. I slid along the kitchen floor in my socks, reaching
for the door, but his shadow appeared. He was already there. Opening
the screen, the inside door. I hadn't locked it. I nearly crashed into him
in the kitchen. He looked around, his brows thick and brooding, closed
the door after him.

"I didn't invite you in," I said. "Get out."

"Or what?" he said mildly, looking down at me with amusement
in his eyes. "You'll kick me out? Call the cops? Better get that landline
fixed."

"Are you threatening me?" Dark terror shot through me.

He shook his head, his face softening. "No, no, I'm just . . . Why
are you doing this? Are you going to punish me forever? Changing the
locks, refusing to talk to me."

"It has only been two days," I said, but it felt like we'd been apart
for a lifetime.

"Who changed the locks? Why would you do that?"

"Why would you keep an extra key under a rock and then sneak into the house and watch me sleep?"

"I didn't sneak. I came home. This is my home."

I said nothing, the fear stuck in my throat. I wouldn't be able to get rid of him now. He had stepped across the threshold. "What do you want?" I tried to keep my voice firm. "Make it fast." *Must warn Elise . . . If I die now, it was not an accident. Dr. L . . .*

I backed up toward the kitchen doorway, where he had stood when I'd brandished the knife.

He looked at me strangely, peering into my eyes as if I wore a mask, as if I'd become someone else, someone he didn't know. He reached out toward me, then withdrew his hand quickly. "Why didn't you tell me?" he said, pain in his eyes. "If I'd known—you should've told me."

"Told you what?" The cold dread inside me turned to ice. I tried to gauge how many steps back to the front door.

"Nothing is a secret in this town," he said, sitting at the kitchen table.

I remained standing in the doorway. "What's not a secret? I don't know what you're talking about." My gaze slid to the wooden block of knives on the counter. He followed my gaze.

"No coffee today, huh?" he said, a slight frown on his face. "You make coffee early, usually. No caffeine for a few months?"

Shit, I thought. "How did you know?"

"Lily Kim, at the pharmacy. I was there buying a tube of toothpaste. I didn't have any at the house. And a few other supplies. She asked me, actually. In a roundabout way. She said something like, 'So, starting a family?' I must've looked surprised, so she backpedaled. She said, 'Sorry, none of my business.'"

"Pharmacists are supposed to be discreet," I said bitterly.

"The test was positive, wasn't it?" he said.

I said nothing, felt a tear slipping down my cheek.

"When were you going to tell me?" The gathering pain in his eyes looked genuine.

"Eventually," I said, wiping away the tear. "I just found out myself. I didn't know before yesterday."

"You didn't call me. You didn't even—you could've sent me a text. At least."

I said nothing, a bitter taste spreading across my tongue. "I didn't have to do anything."

"Have you been to a doctor? Have you had blood tests?"

"No, Kieran! I told you, I just found out yesterday."

"How are you feeling? Any morning sickness?"

"As if you care. I'm fine. But I did faint—I thought it was because I found you with Diane—"

"You could've fainted because you're pregnant." He got up, came to me, tried to pull me into his arms.

I almost let him. For a moment, I could believe he was the man I'd known. I so badly wanted to believe. I was so exhausted—I wanted to lean into him, but I moved away. "Could it happen again? The fainting?"

"It's a definite possibility," he said. "You can't go through this alone. I need to be here. We're going to have a baby."

"No, Kieran. *I'm* going to have a baby. If I don't have a miscarriage. I'm not a young mother."

"Yes, you are. You'll be fine. We'll do everything we can to make sure. You need to start taking prenatal vitamins. I'll write a prescription. We'll run blood work."

"No!" I lifted my hands, pressed them against his chest, pushed him away. "I'm not going to the clinic. I'm going to Seattle to see Dr. Gupta."

"Why? You can see me."

I shook my head vigorously. "No, Kieran. I don't want to see you." A sob rose inside me, but I pushed it back down. I was not going to cry, not now, not again. I wanted to yell at him, accuse him of killing my mother, but instinct, a sense of self-preservation, kept me quiet. I had no idea what he would do to me, how he would react.

"All right, fine," he said with resignation, running his fingers through his hair. "I guess you can't get over something like that so fast."

"Thank you for figuring that out. Now please leave."

"For now, but tomorrow we'll go out on the boat. It will just be the two of us. We can talk—we don't have to do anything else."

"No!" I said. "Leave. Now."

"We'll just plan what to do . . . for the baby. I'll call Dr. Thacker—she's a therapist on the island—and we'll work it all out." He went to the door, his hand on the knob. "Please, think about it. I'll be back in the morning. You don't know how much I love you."

Then he was gone. I locked the dead bolt, then slid down the door and collapsed on the floor. Go out on the yacht with him? Never again.

If he showed up in the morning, I would turn him away. Again. But I felt backed into a corner—what could I do to protect myself and my baby? He would keep coming back, and then one day, he would throw me overboard, tell everyone I'd slipped or jumped into the sea. Or on a hike, he would push me off a cliff.

I imagined mixing the Juliet into his drink, giving him a dose of his own medicine. I imagined watching him froth at the mouth and gasp for breath, begging for his life.

~

It took me a long time to fall asleep. The wind had picked up—every scrape of a branch against the house, every sound, made me think Kieran had returned. But I must have dozed off at some point. I woke from a vague dream that I had floated down the stairs and out to the cottage. The trees swayed in darkness, in shadows, surreal. Next thing I knew, I woke in bed, vague, broken images falling into my mind, the dream already fading in the pale-blue dawn.

I sat up, pulled on my robe, and tiptoed downstairs. The house was eerily quiet. Two coffee mugs sat on the countertop in the kitchen, one with coffee still inside, the other containing only residue. The full mug still felt warm. But I couldn't remember getting up, let alone making coffee. I wouldn't drink any in my condition. Had Kieran come into the house and made coffee for us? But he didn't have a key. I'd locked the dead bolt. Now it was unlocked again.

I must've done it myself, made coffee, gone outside, and wandered around while asleep again. The air condensed in my lungs—the room shrank. Was I going mad? Padding around in the dark, my subconscious alter ego seizing control?

My trembling fingers showed no trace of coffee grounds, no telltale signs of what I might've been doing. And after it all, I'd gone back up to bed. Slipped under the covers, as if I had never been up. My subconscious mind was playing tricks on me, trying to drive me crazy.

Two mugs. *Kieran must have been here,* I thought. *I must've let him in.* I stood at the countertop, my throat tight, my thoughts in a whirlwind.

If Kieran had come over, where was he? Had he gone outside? I opened the back door and stepped out. "Kieran!" I called. No answer. I went down the steps, and I nearly tripped over something heavy, something in my way.

It was Kieran, lying on his back, motionless in the grass, eyes half-open, staring at the cloudy sky.

CHAPTER FOURTEEN

"Kieran, are you all right? What happened?"

He did not reply. I kneeled next to him. He lay on his back, his arms flung out, as if he had simply fallen backward onto the grass.

"Wake up." I slapped lightly at his cheek. His skin felt cool. He did not respond, did not even blink. His hair slid away from his face, pulled down by gravity. He looked skyward, his half-closed eyes giving him a drowsy expression, as if he were merely daydreaming, watching the clouds roll past. But he did not appear to be breathing.

The wind ruffled his hair. His skin was pale, his lips slightly parted, bluish. I thought he must've stumbled down the porch steps, tripped, and fallen, but he would've tumbled forward—he must have rolled onto his back after hitting the ground. He might have hit his head and passed out, but there was no blood, no obvious bruising. No sign of trauma. He appeared to be lying peacefully on the grass, showing no obvious sign of whoever—or whatever—had done this to him.

I was shouting for help now, my voice disappearing into the wind. We were too far from everything. Nobody would come to help. Chantal couldn't hear me from this distance, and the house on the corner was empty. I was alone.

I placed my ear to his lips, no hint of breath. He looked as if he would turn his head and laugh at me, but he did not move.

"Kieran," I shouted again. "Talk to me!"

No reaction.

Time slowed, the leaves fluttering, a hawk arcing over us in the sky. Smells rushed in—moss, grass, lavender. Mint, rosemary, the distant dankness of the sea. And noises—a foghorn, a rustling, a cawing.

I lifted his arm. It was heavy, as if made of stone. I let go, and his arm dropped, deadweight. I felt his wrist again for a pulse, nothing. I kept shouting for help, my voice growing hoarse.

CPR. I'd learned in a class. *Create a V shape on his chest. Put your weight into it.* Fast compressions. I threw all my strength into pushing on his chest, trying to pump the life back into him. "Come on, breathe!" There was no response, no gasp from him, no air intake.

I'd imagined slipping the Juliet powder into his drink, watching him die. But I could not possibly have actually done it. Something else had happened to him while I'd slept upstairs, unaware that he was dying in the garden below my window.

I kept pumping, compressing, shouting, tried mouth-to-mouth resuscitation. His lips were cool, rubbery. No response. I got up, stumbled backward, stars bursting in my vision. I bent forward, head down between my legs, and the blood returned to my head. The stars disappeared.

I straightened and ran into the house, grabbed my cell phone from my purse, raced out into the garden toward the cottage, searching for a signal, wishing I'd had the landline fixed.

The horizon tilted, and I stumbled. The garden wavered and blurred. Nausea rose in my throat, weakness washing through me. I doubled over. My limbs grew heavy. No, not now. Not again. The trees swayed, bending away from the wind. Heavy, so heavy—I needed to dial 9-1-1. *Press. The buttons.* The phone flew away in slow motion. I reached for it, falling. My legs crumpled, the ground rushing upward, and then darkness closed around me.

~

In a twilight world of jagged images, Kieran threw his head back and laughed. Diane clutched the comforter to her chest, jumped out of our bed. *You're gone already. Gone.* I struggled to open my eyes, squinted in the sudden light. Pushed myself up to a sitting position. Cold air rippled across my skin; my teeth chattered. My forehead hurt just above my right eye. I touched my temple, winced in pain, felt a lump. My fingers came away sticky with blood. I must've fainted again and hit my head. On what? There—blood on the corner of the stone garden bench.

The baby. My hand flew to my abdomen. I was clothed, intact, no cramping. That was good. It didn't seem that I'd fallen on my belly. I'd woken lying on my side. No pain in my body, only in my head.

What was I doing here, sitting in the dirt? The sun strained upward through the trees. Dried leaves and bits of soil clung to my pajamas. Confusion clouded my thoughts. My left slipper had come off. The right one was still on my foot. This wasn't a dream. I had been outside all this time. I was awake. Where was my phone? I'd had it with me, or I thought I had. On my hands and knees, I checked the ground nearby, found my phone beneath a lavender bush. Only 10 percent of the battery was left, no signal.

I tucked the phone into my pocket, retrieved my errant slipper and put it on. *Don't stand up too fast.* My legs wobbled, but I was okay, shivering but conscious, lucid.

Kieran had been lying nearby. Now only the garden rippled away from me, the barberry bushes bursting into autumn reds and yellows. A Steller's jay screeched in the hazelnut branches. Kieran wasn't here, but I was sure he had been lying motionless, his skin bleached like driftwood.

A terrible fear tore through me. I staggered to the spot where I'd seen him, dropped to my hands and knees, ran my hands along the ground. This was exactly where he had been sprawled out near the steps. Where was he now? Had he walked away? But he hadn't been breathing. I hadn't been able to revive him.

A garden beetle scuttled off, hiding in the lavender. The orb weaver spiders spun their durable webs in dewy patterns, the multicolored bodies bracing to trap insects and wrap them in silk. Life in the garden went on as before.

"Kieran! Kieran!" I called again, my voice echoing. The surf rushed in the distance, another foghorn blowing at sea.

How long had I been out? The blank spot, the blackness—I had no idea. Had Kieran been here, or had he been a particularly vivid dream? I remembered his half-closed eyes, the cold air stealing his body heat. No breath. He had been here. I knew it.

I followed the path back through the rhododendrons, the rose-bushes, the shade garden to the shallow reflecting pond. I checked beneath every shrub. He was not in the garden anywhere. I kept calling for him. No answer, my voice echoing back at me.

As I climbed the steps to the gazebo, fragments of our wedding ceremony returned to my mind. Kieran gazing down at me with love in his eyes, or what I had interpreted as love. In the distance, Chantal's house was barely visible through the trees. She would not have seen anything from that far away.

There were no footprints in the soil around the gazebo, no broken branches, not a scrap of clothing left behind. An errant bee buzzed by, and a large spiderweb strung between two branches trembled in the breeze.

In the herb patch, one of the Juliet plants had disappeared, a hole in the ground, disturbed soil where the roots had been. I must have come outside and pulled out the plant. Or somebody had.

If I'd actually seen him, his Jaguar would be here. I dashed back through the garden, past the buffer of trees toward the driveway. His car was parked next to mine. The doors were locked. Cupping my hands against the window, I could see the empty seats and console, a packet of tissues on the dashboard. I'd hoped to find him curled up inside, but he had driven here, which meant he was still here. I couldn't have imagined him. I remembered every vivid detail of him while he'd lain in the garden.

I dashed back into the house, the kitchen door banging, yelling for him. My voice sounded unnatural, far away. The refrigerator and stovetop gleamed. Morning sun lit the walls in washed-out pink, the color of diluted blood. The coffee mugs were gone, the countertop wiped clean. Had I dreamed they were there? Or had I washed them? The coffeepot was empty. The clock read 7:45.

I must've been out cold for fifteen minutes to half an hour at most. I didn't know for sure. I couldn't remember how much time I had spent trying to revive Kieran or what time I had gone outside. I'd seen the mugs on the countertop; I knew I had.

"Kieran! Are you here?" My voice echoed through the downstairs rooms—the library, the study alcove, the living room, the dining room. No sign of him anywhere. The antique wall clock in the library ticked too loudly, tapping at my eardrums.

Upstairs, he was not in the master bedroom. Gooseflesh rose on my arms. Electricity buzzed in the air. Nobody was here. What had I done? I no longer knew myself. I did not know what I was capable of in my sleep. But I'd done nothing! Kieran wasn't where I'd seen him.

He wasn't in any of the upstairs rooms. I ran back down the hall to the landing. Grabbed the banister. My voice bounced down the stairs. *Kieran, Kieran.* No response. The house held its breath, as quiet and still as a memory.

Back down in the foyer, I flung open the front door, cold, salty air wafting in. A magnolia tree, dropping its leaves, seemed to struggle to remain upright, weighted by its own widespread limbs. I retreated into the house, shivering. I had tracked dirt all over the floor, soil and grass on my slippers.

If I were to report Kieran missing, what would I say? That I had tripped over his lifeless body, and then he had disappeared? *I'd like to report that I dreamed of a dead man.* I tottered down the hall to the guest bathroom. My ghostlike reflection in the mirror startled me. The whites of my eyes shone. My hair stuck up, my face pale and shadowy. A gash above my right eyebrow still oozed a little blood, but a scab was forming. I washed the wound with hot water, then cleaned it with alcohol swabs from the first aid kit beneath the sink. The stone corner of the bench had done a number on my head. But my vision was not blurry, and my thoughts were clearing.

What if Kieran wasn't dead at all but playing a game, trying to drive me crazy? If so, he'd pulled off an elaborate, convincing ruse. All evidence had disappeared—his body, the coffee mugs. Otherwise I had been dreaming. Or suffering from delusions.

Or I had a brain tumor.

The thought stopped me in my tracks. The sleepwalking. Lucid dreams, and now possible hallucinations. But Kieran had assured me that the type of tumor my mother had was not heritable, most of the time. *Most* of the time. He could have lied. Were the cancer cells eating through my brain even now? How would I know? Maybe that was what he wanted, for me to die of a tumor. Then he could not be blamed for my death. Perhaps he didn't even care about the baby.

No, impossible—I'd seen him. I knew I had. My heart pounded; my head spun. He wasn't in the house, which meant he had to be outside. I found his bicycle leaning against the house beneath the eaves, where he usually left it.

Halfway down the driveway, my phone caught one bar of reception. I hit speed dial for Kieran's cell phone. The call went straight to voice mail. His deep voice startled me, alive and casual, telling me to leave a message at the beep.

"Stop playing games and answer your phone," I said and hung up. I thought of dialing the number for the clinic, but it was Sunday. The clinic was closed.

Where could he have gone?

The cottage. I hadn't checked there. I thought I should've asked Brandon to change the locks to the shop, too. I'd been careful to lock the door the night before, but what if? I rushed out onto the garden path. The shop door was unlocked and swung open a bit stiffly, the hinges squeaking. Someone had tracked dirt on the welcome mat.

The wet dirt crossed the white tile floor, past the glass jars of herbs behind the counter, into the prep room. There, on the wood-block table, a small weight sat on one side of the metal scale, a paper bag of Slumber powder on the other, labeled in my mother's artistic cursive, the ends of the letters curling upward like a vine.

Next to the scale was a wooden bowl containing mixed dried herbs, including bits of the red Juliet flower like splashes of blood. In a white marble mortar and pestle, herbs had been crushed into a powder.

Black ink spread through my mind, blotting out my memory. Combining the herbs, crushing them into powder, preparing a tincture— had I done this?

I picked up the bag of Slumber powder from the scale, and the other side rose up an inch. I removed the metal weight from the tray, and the two trays evened out. I sniffed the Slumber powder, the spicy, earthy smell conjuring a memory of my mother. *Don't ever touch this plant,* she'd said, yanking out the Juliet, which had reappeared and regrown countless times. *Untraceable.*

I pulled on vinyl gloves and placed the remaining herb mixture into a plastic bag. My mother had done the same thing so many times, her nimble fingers tucking the dried leaves away in a sample drawer. Lifting the paper bag of Slumber powder and pouring just the right amount through a funnel into a tincture bottle.

I thought of what my mother had written, that the herb had killed a man. Maybe I had given Kieran the Slumber powder, and he'd fallen into a deep sleep. But he had woken, perhaps disoriented, and had wandered off in confusion. *Yes, this is what happened.* My shoulders relaxed. He was alive. There was no other explanation.

I cleaned up the prep room as quickly as I could, wiped the floor, took the Slumber powder into the house, and hid it in the kitchen cabinet behind the bags of coffee and tea. I thought I should dispose of it completely, but a voice in my head told me to keep it, just in case. Of what? In case Kieran stormed back home in a rage?

I got dressed quickly, covered my head wound with a bandage. Got into my car and drove to Chantal's place. Her Kia was gone. No sign of anyone on the property. If Kieran had taken off, confused, where could he have gone? He could be afraid of me, or at least angry, if I poisoned him. If I did something that I didn't remember.

I drove down through the hills and valleys into town, watching for Kieran all the way, expecting to see him staggering along the shoulder or lying in a ditch. The forests and meadows sped by faster and faster. I took my foot off the gas. *Let up, breathe.* He could have returned to the farmhouse—but without his car? Or found his way down to the yacht. The two other places that belonged to him, possible refuges. He had to be somewhere.

At the harbor, I parked at the curb and walked out onto the floating dock, past a fisherman derigging his boat and a tanned woman washing her catamaran. A seagull perched on a nearby railing, watching me, one stray feather sticking out. Clouds rolled overhead, casting patterns of light and shadow. Bittersweet memories came to me, of Kieran and me gliding on the calm sea as he pointed out the hills on nearby Orcas Island, a harbor seal playing in the shallows.

His yacht was tied to its slip far out in the marina, away from the other slips that extended like fingers from the floating docks. There it was, *Knot on Call* painted in blue along the side.

His dinghy was gone. Normally the rubber craft was tied alongside the yacht. The dinghy was similar to the sturdy vessels that special forces teams used to conduct clandestine missions, gliding ashore in the night. Durable and stable, it was Kieran's tender of choice when he moored his boat offshore and rowed into a shallow harbor.

Had he somehow made it here and taken out the dinghy, or had it somehow become untied from the boat? I climbed the ladder onto the yacht. The deck was damp, but that was not unusual. We'd had intermittent rains. I couldn't tell if anyone had been here recently.

I knocked on the cabin door. No answer. No sign of anyone. I used my key to let myself in, ducking my head as I descended the stairs. The bed was made, the galley kitchen clean. The boat rocked and swayed on its mooring lines. I began to feel a little nauseated again.

I left the cabin, locked the door. Up on deck, I shielded my eyes and gazed out between the jetties toward the sea. The harbor was protected, but the tide was still going out. However he'd managed to get here, Kieran could've ridden the outgoing tide at its height, rowed off somewhere. But where? And why?

As I walked back along the dock, I passed a man preparing to launch his skiff. "Did you see a rubber dinghy leave here?" I asked. "From that yacht out there on the last slip?"

He straightened up and frowned. "I thought I saw someone head out that way," he said. "But I don't remember anything about a dinghy."

"Did you recognize the person?" I said.

"Can't say I was paying much attention. A man."

"Tall, short?"

He shrugged. "Like I said, I can't say. Regular."

"Thank you." I headed back to my car. If Kieran had come here, why hadn't he taken out the yacht? Why the dinghy? And there remained the stubborn problem of how he'd come here. Not in his Jaguar. Possibly in Diane's Prius.

Diane.

She must've picked him up. He had to be with her, or if he wasn't, she had to know where he was going.

CHAPTER FIFTEEN

Kieran had mentioned that Diane had moved to the island to help her dad recover from heart surgery. But I had no idea where he lived or whether or not she was still there.

I swung by the farmhouse—no car in the driveway, no obvious sign of life. I thought of running back home to pick up my laptop, but the library was open for a few hours on Sunday and had its own public computers. It was housed in an old brick-and-wood Victorian at the edge of town. Inside, the rooms smelled of sweat and mildly of mold from recent flood damage. A few locals milled about, browsing the aisles or ensconced at workstations.

Seated at one of the computers, I logged in and searched the internet for Diane Jasper's address. I found several Diane Jaspers in many states, of many ages. When I narrowed the search to Washington State, I found Diane Jaspers in Everett and Cle Elum, but those Diane Jaspers were in their sixties. Kieran's Diane Jasper had to be in her twenties. The addresses then jumped to California, Nevada, Minnesota, Maryland.

A man sat at the computer next to me. I hunched forward at the screen, glanced up toward the checkout desk. The librarian, a young woman I did not recognize, smiled in my direction. I smiled back and returned to the screen, my heart pounding. I revised my search, looking for any person with the surname Jasper on Chinook Island. I found Frederick Jasper, age sixty-three—he had to be her father—on Kingfisher Lane, about eight blocks away.

Up at the house, I parked at the curb. The yard was overgrown, falling into neglect, but it appeared that it had once been well tended—a rose garden in the front beds, an apple orchard on one side of the house. The modern, boxy two-story house was set back from the road, painted in a rich, dark shade of mahogany. A white Prius was parked in the driveway.

I walked to the front step, on which a welcome mat read, Howdy, Stranger! I knocked on the door, my heart in my throat, expecting Diane to answer.

The man who opened the door, wheezing, appeared to have risen from the dead. His skin was ashen, and he coughed as he squinted down at me through the screen. He was handsome beneath the pallor, his mop of black hair surprisingly thick, combed back. *Like a vampire,* I thought. His aquiline features echoed Diane's.

"May I help you?" he said in a phlegmy voice. "If you're selling something, I don't want it. I don't buy Girl Scout cookies, and I've already found the Lord."

"I'm not a solicitor," I said. "I'm looking for Diane Jasper."

His gaze narrowed even more. "She's not here, and she won't be here for quite some time."

"I really need to talk to her. She might have been—she might be having an affair with my husband. Please, it's important."

He opened the screen door, stepping back to let me enter. The interior of his house smelled of fruity air freshener. On the walls were faded army-training group photos—I couldn't tell if he was in any of the pictures.

"Fred Jasper," he said, holding out a large, thick hand. His handshake felt solid and strong.

"Elise Watters. My husband is Dr. Kieran Lund."

His bushy brows rose. He knew Kieran then, had perhaps been a patient. Mr. Jasper ushered me into a cozy living room furnished in plush gold couches and thick, soft brown carpet. In the corner, a flat-screen television, bolted to the wall, played a silent baseball game. He gestured to the couch, and I sat.

"Coffee, tea, vodka?" he said, pointing at the TV with a remote control. The screen flickered off. "I'm guessing you could use something strong."

"Thank you, no. I can't stay long."

"You're looking for my wayward daughter," he said, sitting stiffly, pulling up his pants legs. He coughed again, cleared his throat. "You say you think she might be having an affair with your husband. I'm not surprised, and on her behalf, I'm sorry."

"It's not your fault," I said.

"I find myself apologizing for her a lot. Happens when you've got a daughter into so much trouble."

"What kind of trouble?"

"Oh, whatever feeds her habits. If an affair would help her get what she wants, then an affair it would be. She moved back here to help me, but she fell into her old ways." He glanced out toward the overgrown garden.

"I thought she was a home stager."

"Is that what she's calling herself now?" He chuckled as if the joke was on him. "She is good at decorating. Has a keen eye. I'm not surprised she used that to her advantage."

I leaned toward him, glancing at the family photos on the wall next to the woodstove in the corner. From this distance, I couldn't tell if Diane was in any of those pictures, either. "What exactly is it that she does?"

He clasped his hands together on his lap. "My daughter's profession is her addiction. I'll put it that way. Whatever she can get."

"Do you know where she is? Is there any possibility that she could be with my husband out on a small boat?"

"I'll tell you where she is. She's in rehab again. Packed up and took the late ferry."

I shivered. "You know this for sure. That she was on the ferry."

He nodded. "She called from the rehab center in Seattle this morning. Nurse put her on the line. Saw the number on caller ID."

I swallowed. "She's really there? So fast?"

"Someone pulled some strings. It's not cheap, but she knew she needed it."

"So she has been gone since yesterday?" I said.

He nodded again. "I'll let you know if I hear from her, but she's not with your husband, and she's not likely to be for the length of rehab, around twenty-six days."

"Thank you," I said.

I drove home on automatic pilot. Had Diane been using Kieran for drugs? Had he supplied her with them? But she seemed to believe he planned to leave me and marry her. If she had gone to rehab, then he'd gone out on the dinghy alone.

At home, his Jaguar still sat in the driveway. Yet another walk-through of the rooms, the cottage, and the garden yielded nothing. I got back into my car and drove to Chantal's house, pulled into her driveway. My panic grew. My eyelid twitched. Chantal's Kia was back, parked at an angle next to a truck that I recognized. Brandon was here.

I found the two of them in the backyard, examining a half-built wood deck extending from sliding glass doors to the dining room. Brandon turned toward me, his brows rising when he saw my expression. "You look worried," he said.

"I need to find Kieran," I said.

"He's missing?" Chantal said. "I thought he was staying at the farmhouse."

"He was here. Long story. His car is here, and his yacht is in the harbor, but his dinghy is gone."

"I haven't seen him," Chantal said, her eyes wide with alarm. "So what, he showed up and then took off without his car?"

"Maybe," I said. "Did you see anything? I know you like to go out jogging early."

"Nope, didn't see anything—is he okay? Did you have an argument?" She looked toward the house. "Do you need help looking for him?"

"I don't know, maybe," I said.

Brandon shoved his hands into his pockets. "Actually," he said, "I did see him early this morning. On the dinghy. He was rowing out of the harbor."

Chantal looked at him, her mouth dropping open, then turned to me. "Well—there's your answer, right?"

I nearly collapsed with relief. "Where was he going? When was this?"

"Around dawn. I didn't talk to him. He was just heading out."

"What were you doing down there so early?"

"I was visiting a . . . friend." His cheeks flushed pink.

Chantal looked at him, then began twisting her bracelet around and around.

So Brandon had been with a woman. Fine, I was happy for him. "Do you know where he was going? How did he seem? Was he okay? Disoriented?"

"He seemed fine, I don't know. I didn't talk to him. I have no idea where he was going. He was just rowing his dinghy."

"You're certain you saw him and not someone else," I said.

"Yeah, why?"

"He wasn't with a woman?" I felt all my muscles relaxing, certain now that Kieran was alive, but he needed to be found.

"The redhead? No, I don't think so. What's going on?"

Chantal buttoned up her sweater. "Out on a boat," she repeated faintly. "Imagine that."

"Everything is fine," I said. "I just need to find him."

"You don't seem fine." His brows rose. "Come on. I'll take you home. I'll help you look for him."

"I can drive," I said.

"Then I'll follow you."

Chantal watched us go, her face pale and tight in the rearview mirror.

CHAPTER SIXTEEN

Chantal ran upstairs, gasping for breath, then peered out the window in the hall, toward the blue Victorian. Elise had been hiding something, holding something back. She'd looked stricken. And Brandon had taken off with her so quickly.

Where was Kieran? Had Brandon really seen him at the docks? If he was hurt—or confused . . . She went into the bedroom, her makeup still strewn on the dressing table. Mascara, a light cover-up for her blemishes, the eyeliner. Subtle gold teardrop earrings. The eyelash curler. The soft satin scarf she'd worn around her neck. The cologne, barely a dab. How much time had she spent trying to make everything just right, knowing Kieran would come back today?

Elise had gone crazy. Chantal thought of what she had seen before dawn, the lights blazing in the cottage, when Elise had been in there in a trance in her pajamas, barefooted, weighing herbs and mixing them. But the timing—Chantal had not had her chance to follow through. She could see herself now, batting her lashes at Kieran, offering him sympathy. Reaching out to touch his arm.

She had been forced to alter her plan, to come home and change into jeans and a plaid shirt just in time for Brandon's arrival. Now she would have to look for Kieran, something she had never expected to have to do. She must have seen him out even earlier than she'd thought—before dawn, wandering around in the woods, but then, sometimes kids hung out on the beach and took the trails to the main road.

Downstairs, heart pounding, she yanked on her coat and boots and headed outside to look for Kieran. No matter where he was—coming back in on the dinghy, already back, or wandering around somewhere, she had to find him.

CHAPTER SEVENTEEN

"Seriously," I said when Brandon and I had both parked our vehicles at my house. "You've done enough for me. I can't involve you in this."

But he followed me into the kitchen. "You can trust me. What's really going on?"

The wind picked up outside. I caught my reflection in the window, a dark deterioration in my face. Black circles beneath my eyes, new lines next to my mouth.

"I thought I saw Kieran lying in the garden dead."

In the middle of unzipping his jacket, Brandon stopped cold. "What the hell? Dead? But—"

"I know, you saw him alive. But when I saw him, he wasn't moving. He wasn't breathing. His eyes were half-open. His skin was cold. I tried to revive him. I went to get my phone and I fainted—when I woke up, he was gone." I spoke in a rush, my words tumbling over each other.

He gestured toward the backyard. "So you went out there, found your husband dead, and you fell unconscious? How long were you out?"

"I don't know exactly. Not for long. It was early, and when I woke, he was gone. I thought I'd done something to him. But you saw him on the dinghy."

Brandon rubbed his beard, gave me a cautious look. "Yeah, I did."

"So he must've only been unconscious, right? I should call the Coast Guard."

"And tell them what?"

"I don't know—that he's out on his boat."

"Out fishing or something because you had a fight?" He looked at the healing cut on my forehead, a flash of annoyance in his eyes. "What happened? Did he hit you?"

"No, I fell . . ."

He reached out and placed his hand over mine. "You're pale and shaky. When was the last time you ate?"

"I don't remember. I don't feel hungry."

"I'll make you something." He opened the fridge, brought out hummus and tomatoes and avocado. A plate from the cabinet, bread. He made me a sandwich, handed me a glass of water. "Sit down."

"He could be sick, disoriented," I said, sitting at the kitchen table.

"Be patient. Just wait for him. He seemed like he knew what he was doing."

"But what if he doesn't even know where he is? It makes no sense that he'd just go rowing off in his dinghy. I need to know if he's back. I need to go down there."

"You're in no condition to drive."

"I need to see if he came back."

Brandon sighed, scratched at his beard again. "If you insist, I'll take you down there. Bring the sandwich."

He ushered me out to his truck. The interior of the cab, which smelled mildly of apples, was cluttered with tools and papers. I cleared a small space on the passenger seat, remembering the way I'd always cleaned up after Brandon. Kieran, on the other hand, had been neat to a fault—except when he and Diane had strewn their clothes everywhere and had left their dishes in the sink.

All the way to the harbor, Brandon and I were silent and tense. The wind raged, tree limbs snapping, tiny fir branches flying through the air.

"This isn't a good idea," Brandon said when we arrived. "There's a storm coming."

"I need to go to the boat," I said. "I checked here, but he could be back. Maybe I missed something."

"If you say so." He parked at the curb and we both ran out along the dock, hunching into the wind. At Kieran's slip, the yacht was there, but the dinghy was not back. My heart fell.

"Damn it," I said. "I was so hoping."

"We need to go back," Brandon shouted.

"He could have come ashore somewhere else!" A gust nearly knocked me off my feet.

"He knows his way back. We need to go home."

"No!" I shouted. "He could be stranded—"

"Elise. Come on." He gripped my arm, spun me around as a wave crashed against the slip, throwing me off-balance. I nearly toppled into the water.

We ran back to Brandon's truck. "We should look around," I said, my teeth chattering. My fingers were numb. "We need to check other places where he could've come ashore."

"He's not here," Brandon said, starting the truck.

"He could've lost his way." I checked my pockets. My phone—I'd left it at home. "Could you call the Coast Guard?"

"Don't rush to conclusions," he said. "He's not here yet, but he will be. Let's talk about it when we get back." He set his jaw, his gaze trained on the road ahead of him. When he got this way, I couldn't change his mind. So I stayed quiet all the way back to the house, where he parked behind the Jaguar. The wind crept up from the harbor, rushing through the trees. In the house, the kitchen was as we had left it, my plate on the table, still dusted with bread crumbs from my sandwich. No sign of Kieran.

"I'll tell the police what I remember," I said, "that you saw him heading out, and I thought I saw him in the garden."

"Okay, rewind. Back to the beginning." Brandon shook his head. "What exactly happened?"

"I got up to make tea. Herbal because I'm pregnant." I clapped my hand over my mouth. I hadn't meant to let that slip.

"What? Are you kidding me?" He looked as if his jaw might come unhinged. "How far along?"

"Only a couple of months," I said, blushing.

A range of emotions brewed in his eyes. "Okay," he said. "You got up to make tea, and then?"

"There were two coffee mugs already on the counter. I went outside and saw him lying out there dead." My voice shook.

"If you tell the police all this, you'll be locked in a psychiatric hospital. What will happen to the baby? Think, Elise. Be rational."

"He should've been in touch with me by now."

"Face it. The guy took off."

I picked up my phone. "I need to find a signal. I'm calling the police and the Coast Guard right now."

"No, I said. Don't do that." Brandon grabbed the phone from my hand. "You'll regret it."

"Why?" I said, a shiver running through me. "You keep trying to stop me."

"Because . . . you could get into trouble."

I reached for my phone, but he held it above his head. "What are you doing, Brandon? What's going on? Give me my phone."

"No!" he said, glaring at me. "Sorry. It's just . . . Shit." He squinted, a pained look on his face. "I'm tired of humoring you, Elise. Driving you down to the harbor, talking to you like all of this is real . . . like I saw him get on that boat."

"What? What are you saying?"

"I'm saying, he didn't get up and walk away. What you saw here was real."

His words slammed into me, knocking the wind out of me. "You saw him on the dinghy. You said so."

"I lied, okay?" His eyes teared up, his face contorted in misery. "I lied for you. Elise, what you saw . . ."

"What, Brandon?" I shrieked. "What?"

He looked into my eyes with an intensity that froze my blood. "I told you I saw him get on that dinghy to protect you."

"You're saying he didn't get into the boat?"

"No, he didn't. I didn't see him climb into that dinghy, no."

"Why would you lie?"

"I had to cover for you. You do . . . bizarre things in your sleep. I could tell you'd done it again. When I came over here and found . . ."

"What? Brandon, what?"

"Look, your husband is not rowing away on his rubber dinghy. I lied to you because your husband is absolutely, one hundred percent dead."

CHAPTER EIGHTEEN

The word *dead* crashed through my brain. Outside, the sky had dimmed. "You're joking," I said.

"No, I'm not." His face turned to stone.

"You can't know that. You can't mean it. How do you know? Did you see him? Did you do something to him?"

He pointed at his chest. "Me? You think I did something to him? You really don't know?"

I sat heavily in the kitchen chair, the wind shaking and rattling the house. "What am I supposed to know?"

He sat next to me, tapped his fingers on the table. "I said I saw him get on that dinghy, and that's what I'll tell the police, if you call them. That's what you're going to say, too. If you don't want to go to prison."

"Why would I go to prison? He's not dead. You're lying." I got up and backed away from him, my skin cold. The image of Kieran lying there, ashen, pressed into my brain.

"He's dead because I saw him dead. Because I found him dead in your backyard. I'll show you exactly where he was."

"No, you're just saying what I told you." I gasped for air, the corners of my vision darkening. I couldn't breathe.

He grabbed my wrist and dragged me out the back door into the gale. "Right here." He crouched in exactly the spot where I had found

Kieran and pointed at the ground. "His lips were blue, his mouth was . . . open a little."

The wind whipped through my hair. "I must've told you what I saw." My brain was turning inside out. If Brandon spoke the truth, Kieran hadn't walked away. He hadn't even started breathing again.

Brandon stood, his knees cracking. "He was lying on his back, in brown shoes . . . without socks." It couldn't be. But it was true: he hadn't been wearing socks. "And a white T-shirt and baggy pants."

He'd been wearing his hiking pants.

"And a plaid jacket."

He'd just described, in detail, what Kieran had been wearing. "You must've seen him on the dinghy wearing those clothes," I said, shivering in the cold. A terrible dread rose up inside me.

"No, I saw him here. His eyes were open—he was cold. He was dead."

I pressed my hands to my face. "I don't want this to be true. It can't be."

"I know you don't." He pried my hands away from my face. "Look at me."

"No." I couldn't—I stared at the ground, numb. The worry had been a shadow lurking at the edge of my sanity. The possibility—no, the certainty—that Kieran was gone, that I had done him in.

"It's the truth," Brandon said. "I swear. I found him here. He wasn't stiff yet, but he was not breathing." His face went pale, his lips trembling.

The rain misted sideways, but I hardly felt it. "Where is he? Did you try to resuscitate him?"

"I did, but I couldn't bring him back. I tried CPR, everything. Just like you did." Brandon's voice broke. "But he was too far gone—"

"We need to find him, get him back. Where is he?"

"It won't make any difference. He's floating out to sea."

"What?" I leaped to my feet. "Where?"

"I carried him in a large duffel bag."

"No—how could you? You couldn't carry him!"

"Do you know how much I've been bench-pressing? Your husband was not a big man. I put him in a duffel bag and carried him onto the docks."

"Nobody could do that!"

"Kieran's weight was a deadlift. One sixty-five, one seventy. Awkwardly distributed, but still: easy. I pulled up my hood. I put him in the dinghy. I had a hell of a time getting him out of the damn bag, but I did it."

"Stop," I said, gasping. "You're making this up."

"All I had to do was untie the line and throw it into the dinghy with him. Then I stood on the ladder, on the yacht, and I gave the dinghy a good kick."

"This isn't true," I said, my teeth chattering.

"He was lying there in the bottom, with his head against the rubber side. . . That slip is at the very end of the dock. I was pretty sure the dinghy wouldn't hit anything on its way out between the jetties."

"This can't be happening," I said faintly. My limbs grew heavy again, my face damp in the rain. "Don't do this. Don't lie. Kieran rowed away. He went out there on his own. He got up and found his way to the harbor—"

"No," Brandon said firmly. "He was dead. The dinghy caught the outgoing tide and moved away fast."

The oxygen drained out of my lungs. My body, my mind, felt poisoned. "This is not real." But I knew, by the way he spoke, that he told the truth. He had carried Kieran's body out onto the slip like luggage over his shoulder.

I was trembling violently now. My bones felt as if they were disintegrating. "Why did you do this? It's not possible."

"Anything is possible for the woman I love." Brandon gave me that intense look of pure devotion. The look he had always given me.

"You should've called for help. You didn't even try!" I ran inside the house. The warmth enveloped me.

Brandon followed, maneuvered himself in the hall to block my path.

"Where are you going?"

"I need to find him."

"What are you going to do—search the whole ocean? He's gone."

"You said the dinghy drifted with the outgoing tide. The Coast Guard will find him. I'll tell them what I did. I have to."

"I wouldn't do that if I were you."

"Why not?" I screamed. "You should've tried to help him!"

"Keep your voice down," Brandon said.

"Nobody can hear us! And I don't care anyway." I ran to the front closet for my coat, but he stopped me again, grabbing my arm before I could open the front door.

"If you go to the Coast Guard, and they find him, you will end up in prison, and your baby will be born there. Is that what you want?"

My ribs constricted, compressing my lungs, as if I were diving deep underwater. I gasped for breath, wrenched out of his grip. "How do I know you didn't kill him? I was unconscious. You could be making all of this up."

"I'm not. You did it. The powder was everywhere in the cottage, and you know it. I didn't have time to clean it up."

I narrowed my gaze at him, desperately reaching for a different explanation. "What were you doing here in the first place?"

"I was next door working for Chantal. I got there early, like I always do, before heading over to the construction site. I saw the light on in your shop. I came up here and found you unconscious."

"Why didn't you try to wake me? You let me lie there—"

"I checked your vital signs. You were all right. You were responsive," he said, his face flushing. He slowed his voice as if speaking to a child. "I was going to revive you, but I had to make a judgment call. I could see what you'd done. The door was wide open. The light was on. So I went in. I'd just found your husband dead on the ground, and you were lying unconscious on the path. I thought someone had assaulted both of you. I thought the perp might be in the shop. But you know what I found? All the crap you use to make your magical formulas."

"I didn't know what I was doing," I said, numb. "That's what I'll say because it's the truth."

"You will be confessing to murder, and I'll be an accomplice. Nobody will believe you were asleep doing something so complicated. Do you want this to become a huge deal? You'll be in the news, a murderer with a fake 'sleepwalking defense.' Do you want that for your child?"

My lips were numb, my hands tingling. My lungs wouldn't fill with air. I should've felt happy that Kieran was dead—but instead, remorse welled up in me. "You should've let things be," I said, my gut roiling.

"How could I? I figured you would wake up with a hell of a headache. But the alternative would've been worse."

I buried my head in my hands, then a thought occurred to me. A hope. I grasped on to its fragile thread. "You could've been the one who used the powder—you could've killed him and disposed of his body."

He flinched, a look of deep shock crossing his face. His jaw twitched. "Do you really believe that? I've never walked in my sleep."

"You weren't sleeping."

"I came here to help you. He was already dead. I can prove it, but you know what? You're right. I should've left the body here. I was right to leave you on the ground unconscious. I'm out of here." He flung open the door and strode out, disappearing around the side of the house toward his truck.

"Wait!" I shouted. "Wait. Wait." I ran after him, the door slamming after me, my heart thumping against my rib cage. The rain had stopped.

He stood motionless next to the driver's side of his truck. "What?" He didn't look at me.

"You said you can prove it. How?"

He pulled his cell phone from his pocket. "It's not going to make you happy."

"I don't care. Show me."

Brandon stood next to me, leaning against the wind, and scrolled through photographs on his phone. He stopped at a video. He held his phone in front of me, hit the "Play" button. Birds chirped in the background, the wind in the trees. The light of morning leaked from the sky. Shadows moved over Kieran's pale, unmoving face, lying in the garden exactly where I had found him.

The phone jiggled, the angle awkward, the video taken from above. Brandon's breathless voice came through in the background. "What happened here?" he was saying in the video. "I'm documenting what I'm finding. Dr. Kieran Lund appears to be dead." I watched in growing horror. It had been real. He had been lying there. His lips bluish, his eyes half-closed, staring upward.

"Dr. Lund, talk to me!" He slapped Kieran's face, no response. The camera turned sideways. "Checking for breath. Nothing. No pulse. Starting CPR. I need to call—Elise!"

I gasped as the video kept going—he was trying to save Kieran. "And his wife, Elise Watters, appears to be knocked out cold."

"Stop," I said. "You took video, but you didn't get help!"

He turned off the video, tucked the phone back into his pocket. "I was going to make the call. But then I thought, the police would still find evidence, even after I covered for you. They would still know what had happened. You'd left the damn coffee mugs inside with coffee still in them."

The color leached out of the sky, my head emptying. "So I did see coffee mugs this morning. I thought someone else had been here."

"Who would have been here?" he said, looking at me strangely, as if I had transformed into some kind of monster. "I cleaned them, but I had to move Kieran fast. I had to leave the shop the way it was."

"Why did you make the video?" I said, in shock.

"In case I needed to show it to someone—to you, to prove my point." He swiped through to the next video, which showed him entering the cottage, finding the powder. "This could be toxic," he was saying in the video. The camera swung around to face the ceiling and ended.

I'm a murderer, I thought, the word *murderer* floating in the air.

"Try to calm down," he said. "Try to breathe. You're hyperventilating."

What I had apparently done could not be undone, but I needed to see Kieran's body, to retrieve him. To go to the police. "We still need to get him back."

"I told you. The dinghy drifted way the hell out there."

I ran back into the house, Brandon close on my heels. I grabbed my car keys. "I have to go."

"It's too late now. Report him missing tomorrow. Say he went fishing and didn't come back." Brandon gripped my shoulders, his fingernails digging into my flesh.

"I'm not going to lie," I said. "They'll have to believe me. I was asleep."

"But what about me? I had to make a split-second decision. I saved your life, your future."

"I never asked you to do that!"

"You didn't have to ask! Don't you see?" He stared at me, his expression singular, intense. "I had to help you. It's all I've ever wanted to do. Why do you think I keep coming back to the island?" He kneeled in front of me, looking into my eyes, holding my arms so tightly I thought he would break my bones.

I looked down at my fists, the keys clenched in one hand. His fingers were cutting off my circulation. "You've made everything worse." Kieran had been right about Brandon. He kept returning to the island because of me.

"He was dead. He's not going to be any less dead when the storm passes."

"We have to tell the Coast Guard exactly what time it was when you set the dinghy adrift, and which direction it was going. I'll tell them it wasn't you. It was me."

He got up and looked down at me. "They're not going to believe that. You can't lift a body. Let this go. If he's never found, you didn't do anything. Even if he is found. He's drifting with the currents."

"We need to get him." I wrenched away from him, burst out onto the porch, into the wind.

Brandon came out after me. "It's too late. Why can't you accept that?"

I looked through the trees at the whitecaps churning up the sea. "I'm going. You can't talk me out of it."

"The police will figure out that you hated him. They'll find out about the affair. It's obvious!"

"I wouldn't kill anyone because of an affair."

"The police don't know that."

"I was asleep." I rubbed my hands along my cheeks. "Everything was weighing on me. The Juliet, the journal . . ."

Brandon's eyes sharpened. "The journal I found under the cabinet?"

I nodded toward the cottage. "I read it. She was scared of him. There were formulas for the powder . . . She wrote in the journal . . ."

"It will only implicate you even more."

I turned to face him. "Why would the journal implicate me?"

"It gives you motive for murder," he said. "Revenge for what he did to your mother. You said so yourself."

"But . . ." *No, I didn't,* I thought. *I didn't say anything about the journal before now.*

"Think about it! Your mother even wrote about him. She said he would kill her for sure. Why wouldn't you want revenge?"

How could he know she'd thought Kieran might kill her? "I did, I do," I said. "But the journal is not—"

He jabbed his finger at me, his eyes bright and manic. "You said it yourself. She wrote, *If I die now, it was not an accident.* The guy doesn't deserve to have anyone go to prison for him, least of all you."

My lungs constricted, tremors reverberating through me. A strange ringing in my ears. I had not shown my mother's journal to him after he had retrieved it. I'd carried the journal downtown to the precinct, then I'd brought it home and locked it in a drawer in the cottage. How could Brandon have quoted from it? If he had found it on the floor, if he had not seen it before that moment, how could he possibly have known the exact words she had written inside?

CHAPTER NINETEEN

I turned away from Brandon, dashed toward my car, but he blocked my path. "Let me go," I said.

"Hey, take it easy." He tried to grab me, but I ducked away, charged toward my car again, but he was right there in front of me. He was too quick for such a big man.

"Leave me alone," I said. "I need to go. Now."

"I can't let you just leave. I won't. You'll get into an accident if you try to drive. You need to calm down."

Panic rose inside me. How could I escape this man? If I tried to hit him, he would grab my arm, maybe even break my bones. I couldn't run. He would catch up. He could move fast enough to stop me. What else could I do? Deflect him, outwit him? But how? Try to reason with him? He was smart enough to suspect a bluff. I had to pretend I was not trying to flee from him. Hide the shock on my face. What if I could slow him down? Incapacitate him? The Slumber powder.

"You're right," I said, feigning weariness. "I am a little . . . stressed. I'll make some tea. I've got a calming raspberry blend . . . in the shop."

"Fine," he said, nodding toward the cottage. "Let's go."

By the time I had reached the entrance, I had rearranged my features into a bland expression, belying my inner turmoil. Inside the cottage, I pretended to struggle to find the tea in the prep room. Brandon stood there watching me as I searched for the Slumber powder and tried to devise a way to get it into the drink I'd make him. But the Slumber—there was no sign of it. A wave of panic broke over me before I remembered I'd taken it into the kitchen, hidden it up in the cabinet behind the coffee and tea. How would I get in there, get the powder into his tea? He didn't even drink tea.

I made myself take a breath. Another. One step at a time.

"You okay?" Brandon asked, walking around the shop, picking up bottles, reading the labels.

"I'm thinking about all this," I said. "He's gone for good, right?"

"Right," he said, examining bottles of lotion on the shelves.

"I'm not in danger from him anymore."

"No, never again." He looked at me, his shoulders relaxing. I could sense his relief.

"Good, I'm glad." It occurred to me to test the drawer in which I had hidden the journal. It was still locked. So how had Brandon read the pages? He must've been inside the cottage earlier. He must've planted the journal on the floor under the cabinet, must have read it before he ever showed it to me. But for what purpose? He could not have read the pages at any time *after* he'd handed the journal to me. After reading it in the library in the main house, I'd always had it with me before I'd locked it in the drawer.

I wondered if he realized what he'd done, that he had quoted my mother's exact words to me, words I had not told him.

"You can relax," he said. "Even if they do find him, they won't know what happened to him."

"Why is that?" I said, keeping my breathing steady.

"Well, your mom told me about the plant, too, once when I was over here fixing the light switches. She was pulling out this beautiful flower. I asked her why, and she said if you ate it, you could keel over, and nobody would ever know what killed you."

I had no way to know if he was lying, or if he had read all of her journals. I pictured him in the shop, taking his time flipping through the pages. Finding the information he needed to . . . What? Do away with my husband? If he'd read my mother's dark musings about Kieran, about her fears, he could've come to me directly, could've shown me the journal and let me make up my mind.

Why had I trusted Brandon to change the locks? Because I'd been married to him for four years, because he'd never done anything this extreme. I'd found the journals tipped over earlier, but I'd thought they had merely slipped and fallen like dominoes. All of these thoughts raced through my mind at lightning speed, the dots connecting.

"So I could let things be," I said slowly. "He went off in his dinghy to go fishing, and he never came back."

"That's what happened," he said.

"He took off to clear his head, after we fought."

"You could say he was angry. He was having an affair. You caught him. You argued."

I went through the motions of filling the plug-in kettle with water, turning it on, trying to keep my fingers from trembling too much. "That's what I would say—because that's what happened, right? I woke up and he was gone. He sometimes went out on his own. Not so much recently. But before we were married, he used to take off."

"Now you're talking."

I opened a cabinet above the counter, brought out a blend of raspberry tea leaves, placed them in an infusion ball in a ceramic tea-pot, hardly noticing what I was doing. I had an idea for getting to the Slumber—and getting it into Brandon.

Brandon was still looking at me placidly. "Tell me what you're thinking," he said, sitting on a stool at the counter.

"I'm just trying to wrap my mind around all this."

His brow furrowed. "I'll stay here to make sure you're all right."

"Why wouldn't I be all right?"

"I've just confirmed that you killed your husband in your sleep." That unwavering, sincere gaze. "It will take time to sink in. You need me here. In case you do something you might regret." I could tell, by his posture, that he was not going to leave. He never had been the one to go, from the beginning. Any time anyone had walked out of a room, it had been me.

"Maybe you're right," I said. "My brain is muddled. Everything is . . . fuzzy." Past moments came back to me, but now I saw them from a different angle, suffused with new meaning. Brandon telling me only he understood me, that nobody else could. Bringing over items I'd left behind when I'd moved out, helping me rearrange my apartment. Showing up at the pharmacy, running into me by accident. Coming back to the island again and again. I'd been blind to his obsession—for who would be obsessed with *me*? Insane as it sounded, I had the answer before me. And now the obsession had become a dangerous fixation. He might be capable of anything. Perhaps, as long as I hadn't been dating anyone new, he'd remained at a distance, biding his time, running into me now and then, exercising his patience. But now I was married and pregnant.

"Don't you have a girlfriend waiting for you in the harbor?" I asked, forcing a smile. "You don't have to stay here with me."

"No girlfriend," he said. "How can you even say that?"

"But I thought—"

"I needed to tell you something that you would believe. You should've left it alone. You should've let the story be true."

He flexed his shoulders, walked around looking at the displays in the shop, picking up soaps and sniffing them. He looked so big, muscular, strong enough to lift Kieran's body, to pretend he was hoisting a duffel bag packed with gear. The thought made me shiver.

"You're not dating anyone?" I said shakily. "Not even the woman on the dock?"

"There wasn't a woman there. You know why I went down there."

"Right," I said. *Breathe in, out.*

"I haven't dated anyone seriously since our divorce."

"That's not normal," I said.

"We could've worked things out. We loved each other. We still do. You know what I learned growing up? Never give up hope. No matter what, I made a vow to take care of you, to protect you. A piece of paper, a divorce decree. It means nothing when the person you love is in danger. When her baby is in danger. Even if you're not the father."

"That doesn't matter to you?" I said, a sour taste in my mouth. "That you're not the father?"

"We all make mistakes. You make most of your mistakes in your sleep. Always in your sleep." He laughed and rubbed his beard, the way he did when he didn't quite believe something.

I ran my hand across the metal tray on the old weigh scale. "I must've measured the Juliet plant here and made the formula. That must've been what happened," I said, and looked up at him. "Nobody will ever know. And you're sure nobody saw you push the dinghy away from the yacht?"

"Not that I know of," Brandon said. He seemed to be settling into this imagined collusion between us. "It's the farthest slip. It was dark. All I had to do was tap the dinghy with my foot, like I said."

"As long as you're sure." How long could I keep this up?

"Come here," Brandon said, holding out his arms.

I mustered my energy to go over to him, to let him enclose me in a hug. I forced myself to linger there. He needed to believe I was on his side. "It's okay," I said. "What you did."

He pulled back, looking pleasantly surprised, and relief crossed his features. "You really seemed like . . . you thought I did something wrong."

"I did think that, but I changed my mind." I couldn't go too far, showering him with love and praise. He wouldn't believe it. It was all I could do not to shove him away.

"He did hit you, didn't he?" Brandon touched the healing wound on my temple.

"No, I fell and hit the—"

"The bastard. I knew what he was up to. When he took that woman into your house, your mother's house."

"You saw him?" I tried to hide my shock. "I mean—what, you were watching out for me while I was gone?" Had he been hiding in the woods, watching through binoculars?

"I didn't know you were gone, not at first. I thought I always knew where you were, but I missed seeing you board the ferry."

"You couldn't possibly know where I was all the time," I said, the hair standing on my arms. "You have to work, don't you?"

"True, but I'm good at keeping general tabs on you. I check in to make sure the bastard doesn't do something to hurt you."

"Why would he do that?" I felt as though I were walking on a tightrope high above a concrete sidewalk. I could fall at any moment.

"Hey, he was messing around with another woman. The car he drives. A show-off car, an old Jaguar. Those things break down all the time. He primps in the mirror, in that bathroom downstairs. You can see in through the back windows—he never shuts the door. The guy is into himself, and he's into money."

The heat rose in my cheeks. Brandon had spied on us. Had I walked around naked or partially clothed, left the bathroom door open? I couldn't remember.

"You were looking through our windows," I said, balancing my voice on the tightrope.

"Hey, don't look at me like that. I'm no voyeur. But I love you. I watch out for you. I always have. I'm happy to see you still wear the pajamas I gave you—those flannel ones with the little flowers on them."

"They're daisies," I said, a creepy-crawly sensation on my skin. Had he watched me getting dressed? From where? How much had he seen?

"Whatever."

The frightening idea occurred to me that he could've broken in, could've lurked in the shadows. "Did you actually come into the house?"

He laughed. "What do you think I am? I kept an eye on you from a distance is all. I don't intrude."

"Watching people isn't intruding?" Brandon had become a psychotic voyeur. Who knew what he was capable of doing?

"I worried the guy would do something to hurt you. And he did." He had been watching the house. But how had I missed his truck? It could not have been at Chantal's place the whole time. *He must've parked farther away,* I thought. Then he'd scuttled through the woods. He could've been watching from any vantage point, but he would only have been able to see in through the downstairs windows.

"So you really just got here in time to find him in the garden," I said.

"Yeah, well—I did clean up the coffee mugs for you."

He had definitely been inside the house. "Did you ever go into Kieran's farmhouse?" I asked. "I mean, did you keep an eye on him there, too?"

"The guy needed watching. He took the redhead there, but only after . . ."

"After what?" *After I kicked Kieran out in his briefs,* I thought. Had Brandon been watching me then as well?

He sniffed, wrinkled his nose as if he smelled something foul. "Chantal told me you two fought. So naturally I had to check things out. Yeah, the redhead went to his farmhouse—but she left that night. They had some kind of big fight."

Brandon had been staking out Kieran's farmhouse, had likely hung around there for hours. "What did they fight about?"

Brandon shrugged. "Guys like that, they can't be loyal. He was done with her, looked like. She was pleading with him. But he sent her on her way."

Done with her. Had Kieran been telling the truth? Had he broken things off with Diane? But I still couldn't be sure about the words in my mother's journal, the evidence on Kieran's computer about the clinical trial. Unless he had a good explanation. I hadn't even asked him.

"What happened after that?" I asked.

"He left—took off in that old clunker Jaguar."

"And then . . . did you go into his house?" I said. "I mean, I would've, if I'd been there. To see what he was up to. With *her.*"

"Oh yeah, *her.*" Brandon sneered. "But no, I didn't go into his house. I'm not a fucking criminal. I followed him into town. He picked up Chinese food and went home."

"And that was it?"

"Lights out. I went to my rental—you should see it, Elise. Nice little place across town. View of the strait. But I'm only there until this job is done. Then I'm heading back to Seattle, unless . . ."

Unless. My breath strangled in my throat. Did he expect me to welcome him with open arms? Kieran had slept alone at the farmhouse, when he could have been with Diane. And now I'd killed him—or possibly, Brandon had killed him—and his body floated at sea. "Let's have some tea and calm down," I said. "Oh, but you don't drink tea. A beer?"

"Sure," he said. "I could use a beer."

I smiled, and to reinforce my charade, I kissed him gently on the cheek. "I'll get you one. Don't go anywhere."

"I'll be right here." He sat on a stool at the counter in the shop, drumming his fingers on the wood surface. He seemed almost manic.

I tried not to hurry as I returned to the house. The sky darkened toward evening. I considered making a break for it, glanced over my shoulder. He was watching through the windows. *Just a turn to the left, and I could run.* But he could run faster. The moment he lost sight of me, he would burst out and grab me.

So I went into the kitchen, the clock ticking loudly. The smell of coffee in the air. I brought the beer from the fridge, the can cold against my fingers. I opened the can, reached up into the cabinet, pulled out a glass. Poured his beer. Reached behind the bags of tea in the cabinet, retrieved the Slumber powder. My heart crashed against my ribs. I poured the beer into a glass, closed the cabinet, scooped Slumber powder into his beer, and stirred. Tasted it. Slightly bitter, but not much different from its regular taste. The grains of powder floated like specks suspended in amber, not fully dissolved. *He'll figure it out,* I thought in a panic. *He won't drink the beer.*

He'd never hurt me, in all the years we'd been married, but I'd sensed the potential in him, an obsessive force, like a bulldozer that couldn't stop rolling ahead. I could picture him crushing the beer can, his eyes bright and crazed. He would swing his fist at my head, and I would be gone. I set the glass of beer on the countertop, the frothy surface fizzing.

The cottage door squeaked open, and he stepped out beneath the porch bulb, a frowning hulk. I was taking too long. I stirred the powder, the spoon clinking against the glass. I'd spilled a dusting on the counter. He closed the cottage door, sauntered down the path. The bag of Slumber powder still sat on the countertop. I returned the bag to the cabinet, stood on tiptoes to push it behind a box of tea bags. Then I wiped the counter, smears of Slumber powder clinging to the kitchen sponge.

He stopped in the garden, looking around at the trees, then down at the spot where Kieran had died. *Died. He is dead.* I had to repeat the word in my mind to believe it—but it still seemed surreal. I'd wanted him gone, but I would never have . . . But I could have. Brandon was obsessed, a stalker, but he had not admitted to murdering Kieran. He still shifted the blame to me—either because it was true, and I'd killed my husband in my sleep, or because he wanted to make me feel guilty, to keep me under his thumb.

I opened the dishwasher, dropped the spoon into the cutlery receptacle. He resumed his pace. He was almost to the back porch. I picked up the can of beer and glass just as he flung open the door, dark suspicion marring his features.

The smile—how did I do it? Stretch my lips and pretend to be happy to see him? Somehow, it worked. His facial muscles relaxed, his gaze shifting to the glass of beer. "Thought you might skip out on me again," he said, stepping inside and closing the door after him.

"Why would I do that?" I poured the rest of the beer into the glass, the fluid fizzing again. *Oh no, this wasn't supposed to happen,* I thought. A strange reaction brewed between the powder and the beer—I almost expected the drink to explode. But I played it cool, tossed the can into the recycling bin. Then I gave him the glass, his fingers brushing mine as he took it from me and peered inside.

"What kind of beer is this?" he said, his lips turning down.

Shit, shit, I thought.

He retrieved the can from the recycling bin, read the label. "Hmm," he said.

"You like that one, don't you?" I said. A smear of Slumber powder clung to the edge of the countertop, a spot I'd missed. If he looked in that direction—but he didn't.

He sipped, swirled the beer in his mouth. My pulse in a frantic race, I slipped past him, flinging open the door. Headed outside, back to the cottage. On this stretch of the garden, on the ceramic pavers, I thought again of taking off, but he hadn't ingested enough of the Slumber powder to have any effect. It would take much more than a sip.

He followed me, catching up and taking my hand. The touch of his fingers startled me, as if I'd accidentally swiped my hand through a spiderweb. I didn't dare pull away—he seemed on edge, as if any rejection could set him off.

As we went inside the cottage again, and he casually let go of my hand, my mind hurtled back to a day, not long after I'd left him, when I'd made a terrible mistake. My mother had begun to suffer from headaches, months before her definite diagnosis. I had met Kieran but had not begun dating him. Brandon and I had not been apart long—we'd still been connected by an invisible thread, the marriage still fresh in our memories as we headed down different roads. In a moment of vulnerability, I'd fallen into bed with him again. At the house in which we had lived together, the same Craftsman-style bungalow—so comforting and familiar. He'd proudly shown me his upgrades—a new floor in the master bedroom, a picture window in the family room, a privacy hedge in the backyard. The improvements had worked their magic on me, we'd found ourselves kissing, and then . . . I'd even slept well afterward. His company made me feel less alone, no matter how fraught our marriage had been.

But in the stark light of morning, I'd realized my mistake. He'd commented on my choice of clothing—the sweater too clingy, the pants too tight, although they weren't—and he demanded to know what time I would be "home," as if our brief interlude had recemented our relationship.

I'd raced out of the house, making an excuse, and I had avoided him, not returning his calls for weeks. He hadn't given up. Brandon had always held on to things—assumptions, memories, hope. Me. But now—now he had truly lost his mind. I wondered if anything he had told me on this day was true, anything at all.

In the cottage, I realized I'd forgotten about the plug-in kettle. The water had been boiling for a while. I unplugged the kettle and poured hot water into the ceramic teapot. "Sure you don't want a cup?" I said, the casual tone of my voice belonging to someone else, to a woman far more confident than me.

"I'm good with beer." He held up the glass, still half-full. *Also half-empty,* I reminded myself. *Think on the bright side.* But had I given him enough? He was looking out the window. "Your mom wanted me to work on this place to prepare it for us."

"You mean, for when you were going to move in again," I said, letting the tea leaves steep in the infusion ball.

"Yeah, I did the new floor in the bedroom, painted the upstairs."

"Did my mother say it was for us?"

"Oh, she knew," he said. "She kept talking about how we could work things out, you and me. We were meant for each other."

"She said that?" I said, doubtful. The lies flew from him with such ease.

"I knew it would take a while for you to wrap your mind around the idea," he said, touching a finger to his forehead. "But it was always in your thoughts."

"It's not that difficult to imagine," I said carefully. "We were together before."

"And after," he reminded me.

I flinched, hoping he didn't notice my discomfort. I poured a weak mug of tea, pressed the palm of my hand to the bottom. *He can't really be saying these things,* I thought. *He can't really believe, after all this time . . .*

He lifted the glass to his lips again, frowned, as if the beer suddenly tasted strange to him. *Keep drinking,* I thought. *Come on.*

I sipped my tea. This was a long shot, my hope that the powder would knock him out. I didn't know the correct dosage, at least not consciously, not without checking the journal. I hoped it wouldn't kill him. I needed a plan B, and fast, if the powder didn't work at all.

I wondered how he expected us to go on like this. If he really thought I still loved him, that we were meant to be together, why did he stick so close to me? Why did he try so hard to make sure I didn't make a break for it? And where did he expect me to go?

I'd thought of the island as home, a place to which I would return to heal, to mourn, to start again. But now the island was a prison, the sea's currents its insurmountable walls. Kieran drifted away out there, and I didn't know how much of my suspicions about him had been true. What if my mother, in her normal state of mind, would not have truly feared him at all? Regardless of the deeper truth of his character, he had cheated on me. And yet the danger I had perceived from Kieran paled in comparison to the dread I felt in Brandon's presence. Unpredictable, unhinged, obsessed Brandon.

I kept sipping my tea, pretending everything was all right. That I wanted to be here with him, that I understood perfectly well why he'd moved Kieran's body. The craziness of the situation, that he had made me complicit in a murder—or that he perceived that we were colluding—seemed to escape him. He remained casual and relaxed, chugging his beer as if this were normal. At least he was chugging now, had almost downed the whole glass. But I wanted to scream, to throw everything at him: The vintage bottles on the display shelves. The tincture vials. Soaps. Anything I could get my hands on.

"Weird aftertaste," he said suddenly. "It's got a kick."

"I could get you a different one," I said.

"Nah, it's good." He lifted his near-empty glass. "Here's to the future."

"To the future." I clinked my mug against his glass, fought to hold in my grief and rage. I wished I could apologize to Kieran for racing ahead of myself, for suspecting him of far too much.

Brandon downed the last of the beer. How long would the powder take to work? He still seemed alert, hadn't even yawned. Maybe I had not mixed enough in his beer. Or maybe alcohol neutralized the powder's sedative effects.

"I was hoping you would understand why I did what I did," Brandon said. Were his words slurring? "I knew you would take me back."

"Let's go inside," I said. "It's warmer in the house." The cottage walls closed in, the air oppressive. And my keys were still in the main house. Without complaint, he followed me outside in the garden. At dusk, the wind rose again, after a period of relative calm. In the house, the lights flickered. The next minutes passed in a haze—I could not quite believe that I had spent months, no, years, lying next to Brandon, thinking he was normal. Perhaps he had been stable at one time, and slowly, incrementally, the obsessive part of him had taken over.

In the living room, he sat back on the couch and put his feet up on the coffee table. His eyelids drooped. Time seemed to tick by at an interminably slow pace. The wedding photo now seared itself into my mind—perhaps Kieran's look of love had been real, the way he'd tenderly held my hand. Maybe his slipup with Diane had been just that, a slipup. *Don't go there,* I thought to myself. *The betrayal was real—and whatever else he might have done. Just because Brandon is deranged doesn't mean Kieran was a good man.* And if both of these men were despicable, what did that say about me, that I had chosen them?

After Brandon and I had divorced, I'd visited a therapist in the city a few times, and she had suggested that I'd been susceptible to Brandon's intense romantic overtures because I'd grown up without a father. Most likely, as a child, I craved male attention, having been raised by only a mother. But my mother had done a wonderful job, I thought—I had wondered about my father, had dreamed of him. Yet I'd never felt that my mother and I were less than a family. Until someone had reminded us that we were not quite complete, in the eyes of society. I couldn't bring my father to "family day," couldn't stand in front of the class and fulfill our assignment to read an essay about my father's profession. My mother had been the one to read to me, to teach me to ride a bicycle, to play catch and Frisbee with me. Always my mother. So maybe the therapist had been right about me, that I had thirsted for male attention. I'd had no benchmark by which to gauge the character of the men I dated. But perhaps I'd merely been young and naïve, and I'd chosen, with Kieran, to trust again. To embrace life. He'd let me down.

Brandon's obsession with me was not my fault, either—he'd done this all by himself. As I watched him sink slowly into the couch, his hold on consciousness melting away, I thought about how he used to fall asleep with a beer in his hand, watching the football game. His job had been so physical, he'd drifted into slumber easily, while I'd been wound up after stressful days at the pharmacy, dealing with irate patients who demanded to know why their insurance didn't cover their medications. I had settled into the rhythm of our life together, never questioning our daily routines—until I did. *There is always a breaking point,* I thought.

I waited, hardly daring to move, until his breathing was regular, deep, and rhythmic. *This is my breaking point now.* Slowly, I got up. He shifted, began to snore. I tiptoed out into the hall, step-by-step, to the foyer. Opened the coat closet. A slight squeak. *Damn.* He didn't move, his breathing loud but still regular. I shrugged on my coat. The wind sped up outside, rattling the house. I hoped the noise wouldn't wake him.

I grabbed my purse off the table in the foyer, slung the strap over my shoulder. Deputy John Russell's business card was in my purse. As soon as I could get a signal, I would call him. He could arrest Brandon for stalking me, for breaking and entering. He would have to do something—and he could initiate the search for Kieran.

I grabbed my car keys. Pulled on my sneakers. The front door—when I pulled it open, the noise of the wind rushed in on a current of cold, damp air. Holding the door with one hand, I stretched far enough back to see in through the archway to the living room. Brandon had not moved, his eyes shut. He was still sprawled out as if his body were glued to the couch. I worried I might've given him too much. Maybe—no, I had to leave.

I stepped out onto the porch, pulled the door shut after me. A slight thud, but I'd been quiet enough.

In the distance, through the trees, the angry surf rushed against the shore, throwing the gale into the forest. Tree trunks bent and swayed as I ran down the garden path. The magnolia tree leaned toward me, reaching out its arms. *Stop it. It's only a tree.* Around the side of the house, the wind pushed me back, stealing my breath. I held the strap of my purse to my shoulder, leaned forward, and started toward the cars in the driveway, stark and metallic in the rising moonlight. Kieran's Jaguar, silent and stoic, waiting for his return. My car next to Brandon's truck.

Brandon. Had I killed him? Was he dying right now? But I had to reach the Coast Guard. Maybe it was still possible to save Kieran. And then I could call Deputy Russell, tell him about Brandon. Get an aid car to him or take him into custody.

I was almost to my car, key in hand. I'd have a head start, a little time to get away. A gust of wind shoved me backward again, and my purse strap slid down the sleeve of my coat to my wrist. My keys dropped onto the gravel. I bent to pick them up, shoved my purse strap up over my shoulder again. As I straightened, a shadow loomed in front of me.

No, no, how could it be?

I hadn't heard him coming up behind me, hadn't heard the front door open. But he hadn't come out that way. Something must've woken him—maybe the creaking, shuddering house—and he must've dashed back through the hall, through the kitchen, and run out of the house through the back door.

However he'd gotten here, Brandon stood between me and my car, a frightening giant, and there was no way I could possibly get past him.

CHAPTER TWENTY

I gripped my car keys, the metal edges digging into the palms of my hands.

How had he managed to wake up? Maybe, as I'd feared, the beer had dampened the effects of the Juliet. Or he'd only feigned being in a deep sleep. Or I'd misjudged the mixture. My mother had been the expert at mixing the powders. She knew the dosages. I had no idea what I was doing. Or maybe I'd simply made too much noise when I'd left. If I'd slipped out of the house more quietly or quickly, I could've made it to the car. But now . . . Brandon swayed in front of me, blinking in the moonlight. His plaid flannel shirt had come untucked from his pants. "Where are you going?" he said sleepily. "You left without me."

An echo of our marriage knocked around in my head. *Don't leave without me. Don't go anywhere.* I'd forgotten how much he'd tried to keep tabs on me, circumscribe my life, watch my every move as our relationship had slowly fallen apart.

"I'm taking a walk, that's all," I said.

"To your car."

"I'm walking *by* the car. You're tired. Go inside and rest." I squeezed the keys tighter, probably drawing blood. My heart pounded in my throat.

"I'll go with you," he said, his words bumping into each other. "It's dangerous out there."

You're what's dangerous! I wanted to yell, but instead I said, "I'll be fine. I know my way around." I stepped to the left, but he moved to block my way. I moved to the right, and he moved, too, my shadow.

"You need me to go with you." His voice rose a little on the last word, *you*, almost a whine. As the moon pushed aside a cloud, his face appeared shadowed, and his deep-set eyes looked like recessed, hollow sockets. My heart thudded in my ears. He looked frighteningly zombie-like, swaying a little, his expression slack, his eyes half-closed. Almost the way Kieran had looked when I'd seen him lying on the ground.

"How about you go with me later?" I said, trying to sound cheery, but my voice came out shrill. "You look so tired. I'll be back soon, I promise."

He reached for my purse and pulled, the strap sliding down my arm, yanking me forward. "You don't need your purse on a walk."

"No, I don't. You're right." I let the purse slide right off my arm. Let him take it.

"But you took it," he spat.

"I pick it up out of habit, every time I go out."

Still looking at me through those shadowed eyes, he held his arm out sideways and hurled the purse. It somersaulted into the air, arcing swiftly, and disappeared into the brambles.

I don't need it, I told myself. *Be calm. You're okay.* "You didn't have to throw it," I said. "My wallet is in there."

"You don't need your wallet," he said. "It's dark—you shouldn't be out alone."

"I can see by moonlight," I said.

"Come back inside." He grabbed my wrist in such a swift movement I had no time to react. The keys dropped from my hand, clanking to the ground. I twisted my arm out of his grip, crouched to pick up the keys, but he pushed my shoulder, and I stumbled backward. He moved at uncanny speed, snatching up the keys and dropping them into his pocket.

No, no! "Give them to me," I said, regaining my balance. "Give me the damn keys."

"You don't need them," he said flatly. "You need me. Don't run from me." His words were filled with cotton, as if his tongue moved sluggishly.

"I'm not running from you," I said, but I was. I needed to run now, fast. Through the trees, the lights of Chantal's house winked at me. I could head that way, if I could keep my eye on the lights, stick to the trail through the woods. If I could get to the trail at all.

Brandon's gaze narrowed, his voice a tight accusation. "You're not going for a walk. You're lying to me." In another sudden, unexpected movement, he grabbed my shoulders, his fingernails digging in. "What are you thinking? You get spooked. You're your own worst enemy, Elise."

"You're hurting me," I said.

His eyes widened. He loosened his grip, the wind tossing his hair, but he still held on. "You don't want to leave me, do you?" he said. "We had so many good times. I took care of you."

"You did," I said, trying a different approach. "We loved doing so many things together. Just making breakfast, laughing at the comics in the newspapers. Playing Scrabble." It was all I could do to conjure happy memories.

"I learned how to play," he slurred. "But you always kicked my ass. You never gave me a chance."

I did, I wanted to shout. *For four painful years, we tried and tried.* "Your eyes are closing," I said. "Take a nap, and we'll talk when I get back. I live here. I'm going to come home."

"You loved me, but everything was too hard. I made it easier for you now. It's so easy."

"Give me my keys." My teeth chattered; my lower back began to ache.

"You're safe with me. Don't you see that?" he said in anguish.

"You're still hurting my shoulders," I said.

He let go, held up his hands. "Sorry. I'll drive. I'll take you any-where. We don't have to stay here."

I tried to sidestep him, but he grabbed my arm again, his grip strong and painful, despite the sedative effects of the Slumber powder.

A knife of pain stabbed my lower back. I gasped. "Let go of me."

"Come inside and we'll talk. I love you."

"Get. Out. Of. My. Way."

He yanked my arm, nearly pulling the bone from my shoulder socket. I stumbled, and he threw me down onto the gravel. I lay there, winded. Had he just done that? He'd never raised a hand to me, never . . . What had I done? The Slumber powder must've messed with his mind. Made him violent. But I'd always worried that violence lurked right around the corner for him. That at any time, he might throw a punch—or throw me.

I scrambled to my feet, staggering away from him. Then I broke into a run, sprinting toward the dark trail through the woods. The shortest route to Chantal's house. The moon still cast its silvery light across the landscape. Maybe I would find my way.

"I'm sorry," Brandon called out behind me. "I didn't mean it. I didn't mean to do that." The thuds of his footsteps echoed behind me, catching up fast. He grabbed my shoulder, pulling on the fabric of my coat. I let him yank it right off me, as I stumbled forward and kept run-ning, the cold wind blowing through my damp shirt. My lungs ached, screaming for air. He caught up again, grabbed my shoulder. I swung around and wrenched away—he staggered off-balance, and I kept run-ning, stumbled on a tree root, fell forward in slow motion, and then hit the earth with jarring force.

I sat up and looked back. I couldn't see far into the darkness as a cloud blindfolded the moon. My phone was in the pocket of my coat, left behind somewhere—wherever he had thrown it. But if I could make it to Chantal's place, she could call the police.

Footsteps thumped behind me, Brandon calling my name, shouting at me to stop. I pushed to my feet and took off again, adrenaline kicking in. I needed to remember the trails, the turns. Left, right. The cloud let go of the moon, and light bled across the forest again. I could see, for now—the contours of the trail, the labyrinth I'd frequented as a child, running at top speed. But I never imagined I would be running for my life. The lights of Chantal's house winked in and out of view, but I couldn't tell if they were growing closer or farther away. I could hear Brandon yelling behind me, his voice hoarse and full of rage. "Stop, Elise! Stop, damn it!"

My lungs seized—my heart nearly exploded. I had to stop, lean forward, catch my breath. I could hear him cursing as he stumbled through nettles. The crackling of underbrush not far behind me. I ran again, but I could no longer see the lights. The forest had thickened. I was heading in the wrong direction. Brambles raked at my legs. I'd veered off the trail onto a deer path.

"Elise!" he called out, his voice receding. I had a chance, but where was I?

I emerged in a clearing. The clouds whisked across the moon, then the gray light revealed a one-person tent sagging next to a driftwood log, the ash of a campfire inside a circle of stones. Had I wandered so far off-track I'd reached the state park, the campsites? It wasn't possible. *Thank goodness, somebody must be here.*

"Help!" I said, trying not to shout. "I need help. Is anyone here?"

No answer. No sign of anyone. Somewhere not far enough away, Brandon crashed through the underbrush. "Elise? Elise! Where are you?"

I ducked at the entrance to the tent. "Hello?" No answer. I unzipped the front, crawled inside. In the dim, temporary light of the moon, I could make out a sleeping bag, a portable lamp, a small cooler, a flashlight. Stale body odor hit my nose, the smell of apples. I grabbed the flashlight, turned it on and covered the beam with my hand, swept the muted light around in the tent. Someone had slept here recently. The cooler was open, a half sandwich inside, a juice bottle. A plastic water bottle lay on the floor of the tent, tipped over. The roof of the tent appeared to be waterproof—everything inside was dry.

"Elise!" Brandon called out in the distance. Now again he seemed farther away. Maybe I had lost him. I swept the flashlight beam around in the tent, looking for a phone, a weapon, a two-way radio—anything. A book peeked out from inside the sleeping bag. I pulled it out. It was a lined school notebook, several loose pages falling out, squiggles inside. I thought I recognized the handwriting.

If I die now, it was not an accident. Dr. L . . .

The cursive looked like my mother's. But not exactly. The loops were tentative, the lines shaky. The sentence was repeated many times on many lines. Over and over. But my mother could not have written these words. Unless her ghost had visited the campsite, had decided to write through the hand of a living person, to warn me. But I did not believe in ghosts.

No, these were practice words. Someone else learning how to write like my mother. I lifted the notebook, my fingers numb and red from the cold. My eyes watered—I was still trying to catch my breath. The tent shuddered in the wind—waves crashed against the beach not far from here, flinging up the dank, salty scent of the sea. As I flipped the page, printed photographs fell from the back of the notebook. They landed in a jumble on the sleeping bag.

Brandon no longer called for me. He'd taken off in another direction, or he'd given up on chasing me, or he'd simply gone silent. I hoped he would not find the campsite. If I stayed in the tent, I might be safe.

Unless. Unless the tent was his, and this was his campsite. But he'd said he was staying in a rental in town, with a view.

He'd spied on us, peered in through the windows, possibly even sneaked through our house. Of course this was his campsite, his tent. Which meant he knew where it was. He could find me at any moment—but in the dark?

I couldn't quite grasp what I was seeing—what was going on here? A notebook in a tent, a campsite, my mother's handwriting. Photographs—I picked up the topmost one, glossy but slightly creased. It was a picture of Brandon and me, a close-up taken by the wedding photographer. We must've been exchanging rings or about to kiss. He gazed down at me, grinning, his eyes bright and hopeful. His hair had been shorter, no beard, and he had not yet bulked up. I barely recognized him. I looked young, my face smooth and cherubic, a garland in my braided hair. Naïve. I'd worn soft white cotton, the sunlight bathing us in warmth. It had been a June wedding, and we were under another tent—a big, high-topped white one, in the sun. There was my mother in the background, seated in the front row of the tent—smiling. How happy I'd been, how hopeful. But now I felt as though I gazed upon a different person, not me at all. Brandon and I had been married in the garden at the Port Bay Winery north of Seattle. He'd wanted a grand affair, but most of the guests had been his friends and family. He'd managed the planning, right down to the catering, the types of flowers, the choice of band that played at the reception. I'd helped, but I hadn't been in control.

Brandon and I starred in all the photographs—kissing, dancing, me throwing the bouquet, our friends laughing. There were other photos, images depicting the best moments of our trips we took to Vancouver, Portland, the Cascades. My face smiled out from every shot, our lost past concentrated in the back of this warped, water-damaged notebook. Hidden inside a sleeping bag. But now I saw the past in a new way. He'd planned the trips, gently suggested what I should wear. He'd never wanted me to venture from the hotels without him. It hadn't been a late development in the marriage—he'd exerted his control early on. Why hadn't I understood?

I flipped back to the practice notes in messy cursive—he really had done it. He had forged my mother's handwriting, the way it had been in her last days. But to what end? Her writing had changed over time, growing messier, and in the end, it had not seemed like her own. Perhaps because it had literally not been her own.

What if she had not written those entries about Kieran at all? What if Brandon had written them? He must have. He'd written in the journal, then he'd planted it under the cabinet in the cottage. He'd pretended to find it there, when he'd helped me clean up. The night I'd supposedly sleepwalked and messed up the cottage myself. But I couldn't remember, probably because I hadn't been there at all. He'd been in there, trying to reinforce what he wanted to be true. He wanted me to believe that Kieran had been a danger to my mother. Planting a seed of doubt in my mind about my own husband. Trying to steer me toward believing that Kieran could have hastened her death, that he could have wanted me dead, too.

Now I was all but certain I'd been mistaken about Kieran. Most likely, he had not been a danger to my mother. He was guilty of infidelity, but how much more, I no longer knew. Brandon had manipulated me. How much of my mother's writing had been hers, and how much had been his? He'd written enough. He'd forged the words that had turned me against Kieran. My mind reeled, the horror digging into my bones. I'd wanted to kill Kieran with the Juliet—but Brandon might've been the one to do it. Either way, Kieran was not a murderer. *Poor Kieran. I'm sorry—I'm so sorry for you.* Why hadn't I seen that Brandon was worse than Kieran? A philanderer, a doctor in debt, did not deserve to be murdered. Tears spilled from my eyes, and I found I was sobbing, trying to be silent, but the wind stole my anguish and carried it away.

The air congealed in the tent—I had to get out of there. It seemed I'd been crouched on the sleeping bag forever, but only a minute or two had passed. Brandon was still out there somewhere. Gripping the flashlight, I stumbled out into the cold air—and the light shone into Brandon's face, his eyes half-lidded, his face pale, shiny with sweat.

"No!" I shouted, gasping. "Help! Someone!"

"What are you doing in here? Why are you shouting?" His voice came out high-pitched, his clothes clinging to him, soaked from the rain.

"I read your notes!" I shouted. "You wrote in my mother's journal. You tried to turn me against my husband."

His face twisted with anguish and desolation. He was shaking. "You don't understand."

"You set this up. You killed him. You wanted me to believe I did. You bastard!" I launched myself at him, shoved him with all my might. He stepped backward, lost his balance, and sat in the dirt, blinking, his reactions slow.

"Why?" I shouted. "Why did you kill him?"

"Elise . . . he was bad," he said, slurring his words. ". . . deserved to die."

"You've been camping out, watching me. What the hell is wrong with you? You're a murderer! Go to hell!"

"Stop!" He got up and lumbered toward me, rising like a monster in a tempest. He lifted his fist into the air, a fist that could break my bones, crack right through my skull. I raised my arm to hold him off. He reached for me, grabbing at air. I slipped around him toward the circle of stones.

"I didn't mean to," he said, dropping his fist. "I did write in the journal. You needed to see how bad he was for you."

The waves crashed—the wind raging, blowing a mist of cloud away from the moon. His features were once again illuminated, twisted and unrecognizable.

"Did you kill him with the poison?" I screamed. "You were in the shop! It was you all along! You read my mother's journals. You knew everything!"

"He was . . . bad for you," Brandon said. He raised his hands and pressed them to his temples. "My head."

"He slept with Diane, but he didn't kill my mother, did he? Did you have keys made to the cottage? Or did you break in? You were always good with locks."

He looked up at me, his face contorted into a terrifying grimace. "I did everything for you!" he roared, lunging at me. "All for you. Don't you see?" He grabbed me by the throat, swung me around, his eyes wide, the whites of them glowing in the moonlight. He frothed at the corners of his mouth.

I tried to cry out, but his fingers were crushing my neck. Spots danced in front of my eyes. Only a gurgling sound came out—I couldn't breathe. *My baby!* I wanted to scream.

"I had to protect you," he said. "I had to—"

I choked, pinpoints of light bursting through my vision as I gasped for air. *This is how I'm going to die,* I thought. *My baby, too. The both of us.*

CHAPTER TWENTY-ONE

Droplets of mist hung in the air, tossed in from the sea. My mother's spirit fluttered in the darkness. How I missed her—but here she was. I could reach for her, fly away with her. Float up into the sky.

No, fight back, Elise! she yelled in my mind. *You have to live, for your daughter!*

For my daughter. The baby! She would be a girl. My mother knew. Of course she did. She knew everything, could see . . . everything. Now I could see her, too, my little girl with blonde hair flying in the breeze, running toward me. Laughing in a halo of sunlight.

With all my strength, I kneed Brandon in the groin. Once, twice. He abruptly let go of me, doubling over, groaning. I stumbled away but he caught up and grabbed my shirtsleeve, pulling, and I heard myself screaming.

"Listen to me," he said, swaying, still partly doubled over.

"Stop, let go of me!" I wrenched away, but he hung on, my sleeve ripping. I reached down for a rock from the circle, and I swung it around with all my might, whacking him on the side of the head. He let out a strangled cry, half pain, half astonishment. He let go of my shirt, pressed his hand to his head. I couldn't tell if he was bleeding.

A poker-hot pain spread through my lower back, knifed into my abdomen. I felt the hot dampness in my groin. I was bleeding now—I knew it. *No, not my daughter. She needs to live.* My mother hovered in the trees, there and then gone. Brandon was still standing, impossibly, unbelievably, still moving toward me. Blood ran down his temple, into his eye. Had I done that? Had I hurt him so badly? I looked at my hands in the moonlight, my fingers shaking so much I could not hold them steady. They were splattered with bits of blood. I tried to wipe them on my pants. "No, no, this isn't happening."

I turned away from him and ran. He lumbered along behind me, growing ever closer. I had to reach Chantal's house, but I couldn't find my way in the darkness. *Don't stop, breathe. Ignore the cold, the fear.* My feet dragged, pain searing through my lungs. Thorns snagged my jeans, slowing me down, but I was almost there, faint squares of light blinking in the distant windows. Many turns, up and down, left and right—I no longer knew in which direction I ran.

I stumbled into the garden. My garden. I'd run the wrong way. Somehow, I'd circled back toward home. I could see the fennel stalks slashing against the sky, the house in the background. I was shivering, my teeth chattering as I raced through the lavender beds, silver-edged clouds shimmering in the sky. I couldn't stop—her life depended on it, my baby's life. But my legs buckled, the strength draining from my body. Fragmented images fell into my mind—the waves lapping at the yacht, the island emerging from the mist, the Juliet flowers pulsing like tiny, broken hearts.

Just a few more steps. A shadow loomed at the edge of my vision. Brandon was calling for me, right behind me now. I tumbled and fell into the grass, the garden all aglow. He collapsed beside me in a crumpled heap—his eyelashes fluttering, blood still trickling down his forehead. A silhouette approached me, a man speaking to me in a gentle, urgent tone. *John Russell?* I thought in confusion. But I hadn't called him. My phone was gone, thrown somewhere on the ground in my coat. The voice wasn't his—who was it? The man looked down at me, my rescuer, reaching out to take my hand. He asked me a question, but

I couldn't hear for the ringing in my ears. He lifted me, holding me steady, pulled me to my feet.

"It's me," he said. "You're safe now."

"You're not . . . real," I said, my voice raspy. I thought he must be an apparition, a ghost like my mother.

"Yes, I am. I'm real." He held my hand to his chest, so I could feel his heartbeat, feel that he was solid. This ghost, this angel standing against the light, was my husband, Kieran, still alive.

CHAPTER TWENTY-TWO

Chantal unfolded the local newspaper, *Chinook Island Weekly*, and read the article three times over while she sipped her coffee. She knew the reporter, Dana Parks, a young woman who freelanced as a stringer but also blogged, wrote travel essays, and moonlighted as a crime novelist. She'd done an admirable job, but she hadn't captured the whole story. Her article skimmed the surface: Dr. Kieran Lund, a 40-year-old local physician feared dead when his inflatable dinghy floated out to sea, managed to row to shore ... He had apparently fallen unconscious while out fishing ...

Fishing? Kieran hadn't said a word about fishing on his dinghy. And he'd fallen unconscious, really? Upon returning home, Dr. Lund engaged in an altercation with an intruder, 41-year-old Brandon McLeod, who had reportedly been stalking his ex-wife, Elise Watters, 36, who has been married to Kieran Lund for approximately one year ...

Etcetera. Nothing about Kieran's infidelity, but then, it hadn't been relevant to his miraculous survival at sea. Diane had disappeared into rehab on the mainland, and she likely would not be back. Ms. Parks had interviewed Deputy Russell ("We arrived on the scene to find Mr. McLeod unconscious") and Kieran ("We would appreciate space and time as we work through this—please respect my wife's privacy.

She's emotional and needs to grieve."). Chantal had been mentioned for helping Elise look for Kieran, but that was all.

In the article, there was no mention of the Juliet, which had disappeared from the garden—temporarily, Chantal was sure—and nothing about Brandon's little campsite in the woods. Nothing about Elise apparently seeing Kieran "dead" in the garden. Nothing about Brandon hauling the body onto the dinghy. Elise had confided in Chantal, and Deputy Russell knew what had happened. He and Chantal were good at keeping secrets from journalists, from any outsiders who might come nosing around. After all, Brandon was gone, and Kieran didn't remember his ordeal. John Russell had admitted to Chantal once, when she'd been over to fix his computer, that he'd harbored a crush on Elise in high school. By the look on his face when he mentioned Elise, he had likely never gotten over her, but she was married, for now, and he was unlikely to get far with any woman if he didn't lose the clip-on tie and start doing a better job laundering his shirts.

The day before, when Chantal had stopped by the Clary Sage, Elise had been helping customers find gifts, digestive bitters, tinctures for sore joints, insomnia, skin rashes. She had looked pale, dark rings beneath her eyes, but she needed to work, she'd said. If she didn't try to return to a semblance of normal life, she would dissolve.

I've already dissolved, four years ago, Chantal almost said, but she had hugged Elise, had promised to be there for her, for the baby, whatever she decided to do about her marriage.

Chantal finished her coffee, laid the newspaper flat on the kitchen table, and looked out toward the blue Victorian, winking in and out of view through the trees. The whole complicated, sordid mess was over. But she couldn't help the bereft feeling inside her, the sense that she had failed, that she was alone. Elise and Kieran, together again, heading to therapy, really?

Chantal got up, went upstairs to take a shower. She was still sweaty after her run.

No sign of a sleepwalking Elise this morning. *This should be the end of it,* Chantal thought to herself. Her efforts had all been for nothing. Or maybe not. Maybe her timing had just been wrong, and she needed to rethink her approach. She undressed in front of the dressing-table mirror, pulled on the sexy black G-string, the only thing she was wearing now, except for the shiny lipstick, which she had carefully applied in a thick coat before dabbing her mouth on a tissue. Then she stood in front of the mirror, practiced her repartee, running her hand down her belly. And then she picked up her phone, scrolled through her contacts, and made a call.

CHAPTER TWENTY-THREE

The psychotherapist's office hid in the woods at the end of a narrow, winding lane. When I pulled up in my Honda, Kieran's Jaguar was already parked next to the large log cabin. Our appointment was at noon, on Kieran's lunch hour. I was five minutes early.

In the warm waiting room, Kieran stood with his hands in his pockets, looking out at the trees. He turned and smiled when he saw me, his face lighting up. I smiled back cautiously.

I could still hardly believe he was alive, here in the flesh. Sometimes I caught myself waking in the night, checking to make sure he was breathing. The doctors had found no trace of poison or any other toxins in his system, and no injuries except slight bruising from his fall in the garden and from Brandon transporting him onto the dinghy. He hadn't ever been dead. He had only appeared that way. He was a medical mystery.

I took a seat and picked up a magazine, flipped through to keep myself occupied and at a distance from Kieran. I didn't want to be here, but he had insisted. When I'd reacted to his smile with one of my own, I'd forgotten for that instant the trauma of discovering him in our bed with another woman. This happened now and then but lasted for only a moment or two. On the scale of transgressions, infidelity might fall far short of Brandon's murderous obsession, but it was also far from nothing. Most days, Kieran's hopes for getting past it struck me as wishful thinking, if not outright delusion.

For his part, Brandon would never have a chance to atone for his sins. That night in the garden a month earlier, he'd fallen but lumbered to his feet again. He'd faced Kieran, who had held him at bay until the medics had arrived a few minutes later. They had whisked all of us to the hospital on the mainland. Brandon didn't leave it alive.

He suffered an aneurysm. Kieran and I were not to blame, the authorities said. It was clear we had acted in self-defense on our own property, that Brandon was a danger to us. The police had taken his writings, the photographs, the tent, his cell phone—everything—into evidence.

Would he have been charged with any crimes if he had survived? We would never know.

The trauma of the experience lingered in me, as did the guilt, because I felt responsible for Brandon's death, no matter what the police said. But I tried to focus on hope, for my baby. She'd held on, a miracle. She was still here, growing, and I didn't want my darkest emotions seeping into her. I wanted her to love life, to feel joy.

Kieran sat next to me and took my hand. He was determined to perform his own miracles, to regain my trust. He had shown me notes from my mother, proving that she had changed her mind about the supposedly lifesaving experimental treatment.

And so I had agreed to come here for the baby's sake and perhaps out of a misplaced sense of responsibility. I had not killed Kieran, but I had wanted to, and I had been convinced of his guilt. We could only imagine the way Brandon had been watching us, deceiving us, taking his time. He'd been planning to make his move for a while. He must have mixed the Juliet powder in the shop, must have encountered Kieran in the kitchen alone.

Most likely, when he'd shown up at the door under some pretense, Kieran had offered him a cup of coffee. Perhaps they had chatted while waiting for me to wake upstairs. What had they discussed?

Kieran didn't remember, and Brandon had carried his secrets to the grave. But I often imagined him slipping the Juliet powder into Kieran's coffee during a moment of opportunity, when Kieran's back had been turned, or perhaps when he'd gone upstairs to check on me. I pictured him coming back down, telling Brandon he didn't want to wake me, that it was too early.

I tried not to imagine what had come next, Kieran falling to the ground, struggling to breathe as the Juliet seeped into his bloodstream. Brandon checking for breath, a pulse. He must've thought he had the fatal dose figured, but he'd made a mistake. Then he'd gone to get a duffel bag from his truck, which he must've parked around the corner.

He must've been gone long enough for me to come downstairs and find Kieran in the garden, long enough for me to try to revive him, to grab my phone. Long enough for Brandon to consider whether he needed to knock me out so he could move the body.

But lucky for him, I'd fallen unconscious. How convenient for him, if not for me. And then he had hauled Kieran down to the docks, to the dinghy.

Now, as Kieran and I sat here in the waiting room, it all felt surreal. It surely always would. Yet here we were, on the other side of it, with our lives ahead of us, and the life of our child within me. What was there to do but face forward and see what could be done?

A door opened and an elegant woman in a turquoise pantsuit and black flats, her face angular, her black hair cut into a soft bob, came out and smiled at us, her hands clasped in front of her. *Her previous client must've exited the back way*, I thought. She led us into a warm, rosily lit room behind her—soft carpets, calming plants, plush furniture in muted colors. We introduced ourselves and Kieran and I sat awkwardly next to each other on the couch, Dr. Thacker in the armchair across from us. Tissues bloomed from floral-patterned boxes on tables around the room, ready to offer comfort. "How may I help you today?" she said.

Kieran looked down at his hands on his lap. "We need to repair our marriage," he said, looking up at her.

I let out a sigh of relief. *Good, let him do the talking.*

We told her everything in a stream—about our marriage, Diane, Brandon, Kieran disappearing, turning up again. We brought her up to speed on every detail. She had also spoken to us briefly on the phone.

"So in the space of a couple of days," I said, "I learned that Kieran was having an affair, then became convinced that he was a murderer—that he'd killed my mother, and perhaps his first wife, and intended to kill me. Then I thought he was dead. Then I learned it was my ex-husband orchestrating much of that madness—forging my mother's writing in her journal, making me believe she was afraid of Kieran. Doing all he could to turn me against him. And then he entirely lost it, chased me, nearly killed me."

Dr. Thacker shook her head. "Incredibly traumatic, all of it. And so much to process. How did it feel to find your husband still alive when you thought he was dead?" she said. "I imagine you hadn't even begun to grieve."

"No," I breathed. "It all happened so fast—in hours, really. But it felt like forever. It felt like my emotions were being yanked in all directions."

"I'm sorry." Kieran reached for my hand, gripped my fingers tightly. "I know I'm fully to blame for what happened between us. I take full responsibility. Not that it would matter if she were here, but Diane is gone—she's not coming back to the island. And I'm trying to make things right." He gave me a loving look. I focused on our hands in my lap.

"How much do you remember about what happened, Kieran?" Dr. Thacker asked.

His heel tapped up and down on the carpet. "All I know is, I went over to talk to Elise. I don't even remember going into the house—the kitchen door must've been unlocked. I didn't have a key, but Brandon must have. He'd changed the locks. Next thing I knew, I woke up soaked in the dinghy. I was stiff. I had a headache. The sea was choppy. I was scared shitless. There was nothing to do but try to row to shore." Kieran took a deep, shuddering breath. His face had paled. "He could've just taken me out and thrown me overboard. Why the hell didn't he?"

"He didn't know how to operate your yacht," I said. "Or maybe he wanted your body to be found, so I wouldn't be looking for you. So he could be with me." A shiver ran through me.

"You don't remember anything else about that day?" Dr. Thacker asked Kieran.

He shook his head. "It took me a while to row into the harbor against the tide, and then I hitched a ride home. My phone was gone. I couldn't get through to Elise. I wish I could've been there for her. I had no idea what he'd done, using that powder."

"The 'Juliet,'" Dr. Thacker said, checking her notes. "Do you think that's why your mother named it that? Like what Juliet took in *Romeo and Juliet*? Causes people to seem like they're dead, at a certain dose, but they wake up?"

"I imagine so," I said. I'd thought my mother had chosen to name the plant after her middle name, but the reason had been far more sinister.

"Dangerous stuff," Dr. Thacker said. "But then, I imagine so many plants are."

"I pulled it out. But it could come back."

"It was lucky Brandon didn't give me quite enough to kill me," Kieran said, rubbing his head.

"He probably thought he knew the dosage," I said. "But my mom's writings were confusing."

Dr. Thacker sipped from a glass of water. "Well, as I say, this is all an enormous amount to work through. If you both seek out someone to talk to on your own, great. Our focus here will be on the two of you, as a couple. We'll keep talking here if you're willing."

"The baby's coming whether we like it or not," I said. "But I'm not sure if I want to stay in this marriage."

Kieran gave me a stricken look, squeezed my hand even tighter. "I want to be with you."

I stiffened and went on, "I'm thinking about what I want to do. Stay or move away, be single, put everything behind me. I love the house, the shop . . ."

"I love you and the baby," Kieran said, his eyes glistening with tears. "I'll do anything."

"This is a big decision," Dr. Thacker said, "and a tough one to make at such a fraught time. Have you considered staying together for now, around the birth of the baby? That can be a hard time to be alone."

"All right." I nodded, agreeing, not looking at Kieran. He had also offered to remove himself from my will. I had altered certain clauses, but he still stood to inherit a substantial portion of my estate—for the care and education of our child until she was old enough to manage her own funds. I reminded myself that agreeing to a few months in therapy didn't mean I would stay with him forever. It only meant our child's parents would be together for her birth.

When we left Dr. Thacker's office, I felt a glimmer of hope. I couldn't deny the relief I'd experienced when Kieran had reappeared that night, taking my hand.

~

We kept going to therapy, once a week, and as the months passed, the trauma of those September days slowly fell away. I focused on my customers in the shop. I attended fund-raisers for the town garden, the library, the community center. I put on weight, my belly growing by the day. My feet began to hurt at work—my lower back, too.

After a while, I couldn't lie on my side in bed anymore. Kieran took care of me, rubbing my feet, bringing me pillows, and we returned to a fragile sense of normalcy. Occasionally, when his cell phone rang, and he answered in a low voice, my antennae went up. But he would always smile, tuck the phone away, and come over to reassure me. Everything was okay now. I could trust him.

CHAPTER TWENTY-FOUR

"She's asleep," Kieran said, placing Bella gently in the bassinet. He gazed down at her with adoration in his eyes. "She's so beautiful. Just like her mom."

"Thank you, but you can't tell what she's going to look like," I whispered, leaning back against four pillows. "She's only three weeks old."

"No, I can tell. She has your nose."

"And your ears," I said. "Very clearly your ears."

"Your hands in miniature."

"They're cool hands, don't you think?"

"And she's fussy like you," he said.

"All babies are fussy," I said. But Kieran had the touch. He could quiet her so easily. I was so tired of trying, I could hardly move. Fatigue cut to my bones. I'd been up every two hours for what seemed like forever. Feeding her, burping her, changing her, holding her. Watching every facial expression, every movement.

Our lives before Bella's birth felt like a distant, fuzzy dream of luxurious nights spent actually sleeping. She was all-consuming, exhausting. She took every space in my head, every ounce of my attention. But this was a blessing. I no longer dreamed of Brandon chasing me in the woods, grabbing my neck. But sometimes, when something reminded me of him, when I drove past a new construction project, I also felt a certain melancholy. I had once loved him, and in his mind, peering in through our windows, sneaking into our house, and trying to kill my husband had all been done out of love, because he cared for me in his twisted way.

But now the wonder of Bella's smile, of her entire being, sent the past running for cover. When I looked into her cherubic face, I wondered how the world could ever have existed without her.

A July breeze wafted in through the window, carrying the exquisite, sweet smell of the flowering privet hedge. I looked around at the library that had become our temporary bedroom on the first floor, as I still had trouble climbing the stairs without pain. Kieran had set up our bed in here, had moved in the bassinet. I'd grown accustomed to falling asleep surrounded by shelves of books.

He reached over to adjust the pillows behind my head. "Anything else I can get you?"

I took his warm hand, and he sat beside me on the mattress. "You're so helpful. I should be able to move back upstairs soon."

"You need to heal," he said, resting his hand on my belly. "Let me see the incision."

I lifted my shirt to show him the scar across my abdomen, a little under a foot long. I hadn't realized I had so much skin. The staples had been removed, and I no longer tucked a sanitary napkin between my skin and the elastic waistband of my sweatpants. The chafing had been unbearable during the first few days. "Does it look okay, doc? Do I pass muster?"

"Everything's A-okay," he said. "Looks like you're healing well. Any pain?"

"Only when I stand up. I get a twinge, but it goes away. I'm sick of being stuck down here, much as I love all these gardening books."

"You could climb stairs if you take it easy. There's no law against it. But you never take it easy. That's the problem."

"It's in my nature to push," I said, gripping his hands in both of mine. "Come to bed. It's almost seven."

"Seven!" he said, laughing. He nodded toward Bella. "That used to be dinnertime."

"Dinner, breakfast. Night, day. It's all the same now. You need some rest."

"Soon." He stood, waved his phone. "I have to check my messages."

I groaned. Even now, when he had been so loyal, by my side these last months, I felt a touch of unease. "Hurry back—do you have to be on call?"

"Not often," he said, bending down to kiss me tenderly on the lips. "I could say I won't do it anymore. Because of Bella."

"You would do that?"

"I would do anything."

"No, your patients need you," I said. "Go ahead."

"We'll take another walk in the morning?" he said brightly. "You need to keep exercising."

"I am," I said. "I got out of bed and walked only twelve hours after surgery, remember." Not that the C-section had felt like surgery. It had all gone much faster than I had expected—the prep, the spinal, and then the delivery—although Bella's birth had felt violent, unnatural. The table on which I'd lain had been shaking, and I could feel the pressure and tugging when the doctors had wrenched her from my womb. But we'd had no choice. She was breech. Kieran had been holding my hand the whole time, the anxious husband, not the doctor performing the surgery.

"You push yourself too hard," he said again, checking Bella one more time. "That's why I have to go with you when you head off down the garden path, to make sure you don't run a marathon." When we took short walks, he carried Bella against his abdomen in the tactical carrier, which looked like a bulletproof vest.

"I couldn't if I tried. Come right back, okay?"

"Always."

When he left, my breath still caught. I sometimes worried he wouldn't come back. I could still remember the way he'd looked, lying in the garden, his skin ashen, when I thought I'd lost him. I exhaled now, closed my eyes, listened to the crackle of gravel as he walked down the driveway through the summer night, to find a signal on his phone. Our marriage still hung by a fragile thread, but we would have to keep trying. Nothing was ever easy.

My muscles felt tight—I needed to stretch. I'd made a tentative start with tai chi, when I could catch a few minutes. I opened my eyes, threw off the sheets, rolled over, and pushed myself up to a sitting position. I still couldn't engage my abdominal muscles to twist upright without a spasm of pain. I stood and leaned over the bassinet to check on Bella. She slept peacefully, but I knew it wouldn't last.

The night was cooling off now, the breeze carrying a summer chill. *Only in the Pacific Northwest,* I thought. I closed the window, hoped Bella's sleeper would keep her little toes warm. The flannel sheet would help, and I felt tempted to tuck a blanket around her, but it was too dangerous. I'd had nightmares of the covers suffocating her.

I turned up the wall thermostat by a couple of degrees—it was strange to have to warm the house in summer, but we were on the windy side of the island. Where was my sweater? I looked around. Kieran had just done laundry, had put away my clothes in my dresser upstairs.

I checked through the folded shirts and pants he'd placed on shelves by the bed. No sweater. After a few minutes, he didn't return. I hated relying on him—helplessness didn't suit me. But he never complained about pulling his weight. *Bella is my child, too.* He had come through for me, shopping, cleaning, doing the heavy lifting. Caring for her.

His phone calls were taking a while. After another ten minutes, I thought, *Screw it, I'm not going to wait anymore.* I would get my own sweater, even if it meant climbing the stairs. I was sick of feeling like an invalid.

"Daddy said I could do it," I told Bella. "I can climb stairs if I want." I turned on her monitor, made sure the remote video of her face appeared on my phone through the wireless internet connection. I could look at my iPhone screen and see her every movement in the bassinet.

Each step to the second floor gave me a twinge. I took the stairs one at a time. Finally, I made it to the top. It was nice to be in the master bedroom again. We were starting anew. Except for the yawning space where the bed should have been. Kieran had painted the walls a soothing light blue, and the furniture was all new, too, made of distressed, reclaimed wood. There was no trace of the bedroom in which I had caught him in bed with Diane. This was a different space altogether now. We had transferred the antique dresser and bureau into the guest room. Bella's nursery, down the hall, would wait until I could move back upstairs.

All this, although I had never expected to stay with Kieran at all. I still couldn't really believe it, but I had needed him through the pregnancy, and I needed him even more now. His coat was draped over my dresser, hanging down over the drawers. I lifted it to move it out of the way, and a faint perfume wafted into my nose. I sniffed along the fabric until I found the source of the scent, a spot on the lapel. A familiar fragrance, but I couldn't place it.

My throat tightened—my antennae went on high alert. I looked at the app on my phone. Bella still slept peacefully. Kieran wasn't back yet. I checked the exterior pockets of his coat, found a few coins, a crumpled tissue, a rubber band. There were two inside pockets. One was empty. I pulled a folded napkin out of the other one, from the Starfish, the pub downtown. I almost tucked the napkin back into his pocket, but then I unfolded it. Written inside was the name *Alexa* and a local telephone number, and then, *Call me.*

Alexa. I remembered the name tag on a soft red blouse, on the waitress at the Starfish. Kieran and I had been in there a few times in the last several months, to pick up desserts I'd been craving. Alexa glided everywhere, balanced drinks and desserts on trays with ease as she wove around the tables, flashing her movie-star grin. I remembered her because she was perfect, like an android woman created from a fantasy— straight white teeth, luminous amber hair, and a ballerina's body. She was barely eighteen, and she was in fact a dancer, heading off to college in the fall, hoping to be accepted into the Pacific Northwest Ballet School. She'd told us once when Kieran had asked where she'd come from, since we hadn't seen her before. She'd moved in with her dad on the island, she'd said, just until school started in September. She'd been living with her mother in Spokane, but they weren't getting along.

I looked at the name again, *Alexa*, written in a looping, immature cursive, and my hand began to shake. I imagined Kieran stopping in to the Starfish for cheesecake, a drink, tossing her his charming grin. He had captured her with his blue-eyed gaze, those shoulders. It would never end.

Numb now, I tucked the napkin into my pocket. When had Alexa given him her number? Recently, or had her overture initiated an affair days or weeks earlier?

My incision suddenly throbbed. My joints ached—my whole body felt heavy. I wanted to close my eyes and blot out reality, but instead I checked the pockets of the pants he had recently worn, draped over a chair. Pulled out a small, flat package from his back pocket. An unopened condom.

CHAPTER TWENTY-FIVE

I was downstairs by the time Kieran returned, but not in bed. Bella was awake. I'd nursed her, and now I sat in the rocking chair, holding her swaddled in my arms. "You're still alive," I said. "Surprise."

"That took forever," he said, putting his phone on the desk.

"Someone in trouble?" I said. "Emergency?"

"Yeah, nothing for you to worry about. How is our little beauty?" He emptied the pockets of his pants, putting his wallet, coins, and crumpled receipts on the desk.

"She was hungry," I said.

He looked at me, did a double take. "What's wrong? You're crying."

"Yes, I am," I said softly. It didn't help that my hormones had already sent my mood swinging in all directions. "I went upstairs."

I could see a slight flicker in his eyes, then he broke into a smile. "That's good. You made it all the way with no pain?"

"It hurt a little."

"We can move up there again soon, then?"

"Who's Alexa?" I said, unfolding the napkin from my pocket, holding it up in the air.

He feigned confusion, his brow furrowing. Took the napkin from me, pretended to read the words for the first time. "What's this?" he said, looking at me, his gaze clear and direct.

"I found it in your coat pocket."

"What coat?" He didn't even blush, didn't break a sweat.

"The one you draped over my dresser."

"The trench coat? Oh—that's right. I took a napkin from the Starfish, but I didn't read what was on it."

"That's funny—you must've been flirting with her. With Alexa."

"With Alexa! Who's that?"

"Don't pretend you don't know."

"The waitress," he said thoughtfully. He ripped up the napkin in a great theatrical show, threw it into the recycling bin. "She has a crush on me. It's awkward. I had no idea she'd written anything on the napkin."

But he knew. I knew he did. "You were in there without me. She gave you her number. She must've had a reason to believe you would want it. Did you flirt with her? Ask her out?"

"What? Hell no." He came to kneel beside me. "You and Bella are everything to me. You know that."

"This therapy we've been doing," I said. "It's based on the idea that people can change. But you don't, that's for sure. Is it like a reflex for you? You can't help yourself?"

He stood abruptly, his eyes suddenly flat, but he spoke in the same soft, plying voice. "You're reading too much into a number on a napkin. Alexa's a kid. She's infatuated. Would I throw everything away for some teenager?"

"A beautiful teenager, who's conveniently over eighteen," I said. "Are you sleeping with Diane again, too?"

"What? No. She's gone—"

"Out of rehab, living in Seattle, so you needed someone new."

He reached down to touch Bella's cheek, his eyes brimming with love. "She's my joy," he said, then he looked up at me, the familiar, beseeching look in his eyes. "So are you. Postpartum depression can be a strong destructive force. It can bring out suspicions, make you question reality. It's completely normal. Almost eighty-five percent of all women experience some sadness after—"

"Stop turning this around on me."

He touched my cheek tenderly, but I flinched away. "You see things that aren't there," he said. "You're paranoid."

"*I'm* paranoid!" I could feel Bella squirming. I took a deep breath, exhaled.

"Let me take her," he said, lifting her into his arms, supporting her head. I reached for her, utter fear flashing through me. She was so small, so fragile.

"No, give her back!" I said.

"I'm not going to hurt her," he said, cradling her. "Take it easy."

My insides twisted into tight knots. "Give her to me."

She was fussing now. "She's fine. She's my sweet booboo, aren't you, Bella Booboo?" He gently placed her back in the bassinet. "You know your daddy loves you and your mommy more than anything. Even if Mommy is losing her mind."

"My mind is in fine working order." I reached into my sweater pocket, produced the small package I'd found in his pants pocket upstairs, threw it onto the bed.

He looked at the package, then at me. "What's that?"

"I also found that in your pants pocket," I said. A sad weariness settled into me, a sense of finality. There was no going back for us now.

He laughed, picked up the condom off the bed, and threw it into the garbage. "You've got to stop snooping. You're losing it. That was in my pocket forever. It probably got washed a hundred times."

"That's ridiculous. You're lying." He could make anything he said, no matter how outlandish, sound like the truth. That was his gift, his ability to persuade people with his charm, to explain anything away. He could make me question myself. Chip away at my certainty. "Why was the condom in your pocket, Kieran?"

"Why wouldn't it be? I've always carried one in case we needed it, but we haven't needed it lately. I thought . . . you know, you wouldn't want to get pregnant again too soon. Your body needs a rest."

I swallowed my reply, not wanting any more lies. He would've kept the entire box of condoms in the nightstand, easily reached, if he were telling the truth. I was not yet ready, anyway, so soon after Bella's birth. Sex was the furthest thing from my mind, but not, evidently, from his.

"Look," he said gently. "We'll talk. I'll make you the usual? Organic ginger turmeric tea?"

I nodded, sighing. I wanted him out of the room so I could think about what to do. *You're okay, you will survive,* I told myself when he'd left. I heard him clanking around in the kitchen, whistling carelessly, as if I had not just accused him of a second round of infidelity. But I was the sucker this time. *Fool me once, shame on you. Fool me twice . . .* I thought of Brandon's words in the woods that night. He'd tried to warn me. *He's bad for you.* Even in his psychotic obsession, he had spoken the truth.

I picked up my phone from the desk, scrolled through my contacts list to Dr. Thacker's number. *We're canceling our next appointment,* I would say when I called.

Have you considered staying together for now, around the birth of the baby? Dr. Thacker had said that in our first session. *That can be a hard time to be alone.* I had agreed to this, to wait, to give Kieran a second chance. He had slipped up once. He hadn't killed anyone. I'd felt such terrible guilt for suspecting him of such a heinous act. No, in that, he'd been the victim.

Therapy had done nothing to change him. *Emotions, feelings, communication.* So important, right? It was all bullshit. There was no good reason for what he'd done, but I'd agreed that we would work on our marriage—no, *I* had worked on our marriage, while Kieran had gone on being his lecherous, deceptive self.

I put down the phone. No signal. The landline worked in the hall now. I would make the call from there, later. I would seek her advice about the easiest, smoothest way to split up with Kieran. He still insisted on returning calls from his cell phone—now I better understood why. He wasn't always calling his patients.

He returned with my cup of tea and a slice of banana bread. "Good for the nursing mom," he said. He held Bella and walked around with her while I sipped my tea and ate the bread and mustered the courage to say what I needed to say.

"You will always be Bella's dad," I told him finally. "And I'm glad you were around for her, for us. But I can't do this anymore. Cheating is cheating." I took in his wavy russet hair, shiny, with strands of gold. His broad shoulders, those eyes that could be soft and caring, or hard and distant. I never knew which expression was really him—who was the real Kieran? It didn't matter. I'd given him a second chance. He didn't get a third.

"What are you talking about?" he said, not looking at me, bouncing the baby gently against his chest. He was a good father, for now.

"I want a divorce," I said. "I won't try to keep Bella from you. We'll have to share her. Somehow. But I can't be with you anymore."

He stopped bouncing her and turned around to face me, his eyes sad. "That's what I thought you might say."

"I tried, I really did. I agreed to go to marriage counseling with you. But it's over."

"I was afraid of this. I can't argue with you. I'm so sorry." He came close to the bed, his shadow falling over me. He held Bella tenderly in his arms, kissed her forehead.

I fell back against the pillows again. I was so, so tired of all this. I felt as if a dial had been turned up, increasing gravity's pull on my limbs. On my eyelids, too. So he understood. We would discuss the details later, the arrangements. Now, maybe finally, sleep would come.

"Check if she needs a diaper change," I said. The words thick, as though I'd just had dental work done.

Kieran sat beside me. I could feel the mattress depressing beneath his weight, smell his subtle cologne—and Bella's baby powder. He placed her in the bassinet, reached out to touch my forehead. "I'll change her," he said. "Are you okay? You look pale."

"I'm so . . . tired." My eyelids drooped. The room blurred—the soft cadence of the waves drifted in through the window.

"That's the tea," he said. "And the banana bread." He turned off the bedside lamp.

"The . . . bread?" My thoughts tangled up. Bread couldn't make a person sleepy, and the ginger turmeric tea settled the stomach. It didn't make . . . a person . . .

"The Juliet is in both. In the tea and in the bread. A double dose. A risk, but . . . the cops never completely believed in the power of the Juliet. But we know better, don't we?"

The Juliet. An alarm bell rang in my mind, but far away, across a vast and impossible expanse. *No, Bella. I can't leave her.*

I must've spoken her name aloud, because he replied, "I'll take good care of her." I could feel his cool fingers caressing my forehead. "You don't have to worry. She's my flesh and blood."

No, not Bella. Not my baby. But I couldn't scream. My vocal cords were stuck. *Must. Save her.*

"Go to sleep," he said gently, in the distance. "Just like your mom. She went to sleep." I could see him, the fuzzy shape of him through my half-closed eyelids.

"You killed her!" I tried to shout, but the words came out a whisper, barely audible. I could not say more—my tongue had swelled in my mouth, pressing down into my throat.

"That word. It was an easy death. But I didn't use a plant. I didn't actually know about the Juliet back then. Brandon made up that part.

But I did use an anesthetic. Also not traceable. But no, I didn't 'kill' her. I simply helped her along the path she was already taking."

"No . . ." My eyelids fluttered shut. Why couldn't I move? *My poor mom.* Brandon had been right. He'd tried to warn me.

"I'm sorry this took so long," Kieran was saying. "But now is as good a time as any. I needed to use the Juliet, if only for poetic justice. You and your ex-husband—your lover, I'm sure—conspiring to kill me with that fucking plant. I know you were in on it with him."

No, I wasn't, I said in my mind. *It was Brandon. Just give me Bella. My baby.*

"Now you get a dose of your own medicine," Kieran went on. "I have Chantal to thank for the formula. I've got no fucking idea how to crush herbs and mix witches' potions." He caressed my cheek, his touch a burn.

"No!" I managed to blurt. *Chantal.* The perfume on his lapel. Her floral scent. Really? My friend? Chantal had pretended to care about me. Had pretended to dote on Bella. I lifted my arm with all my strength, whacked him away. But my attempt was feeble. I reached for Bella—where was she? Had he picked her up out of the bassinet? I collapsed back onto the bed, exhausted, my body as heavy as a boulder.

"Don't try to move," Kieran said gently. "It will only make things worse."

"No." Had I spoken, or only thought the word?

"Chantal said it might take a little time. She knew how to interpret your mother's recipe. She just made it stronger than whatever concoction you and Brandon conjured up to kill me."

But I didn't kill you, I thought. *It wasn't me. Chantal. Not Chantal!*

I must've spoken aloud again. "Yes," he said, "Chantal. She came on to me. Pretty relentlessly."

His voice receded. Bella floated away from me. *No. My baby. No!*

"I've got an excellent babysitter lined up, so don't worry," he said. "I love you, Elise, but you're so . . . demanding. You want everything your way. You're insecure and unstable. I wanted to make our marriage work, but you'll always be crazy and paranoid. When I get the estate squared away, Bella and I, we're moving to the city. I hope you don't mind. I'm sick of this island. It's so fucking boring."

Don't take her. Don't take Bella! I screamed inside. My eyes were glued shut, a concrete weight crushing my chest. I could hear Kieran zipping up a bag in the distance, cooing to Bella.

"Don't worry about our baby," he said, close to my ear now. "I could never hurt her. She's so much like me. She'll be safe with the babysitter tonight, and then she will grow up with me."

No—never! I wanted to scream, but I had no voice, and my silent cry turned inward.

"I'm afraid Bella and I—we can't stay," he said. "I've got a prior engagement. With Chantal, not Alexa. Alexa was a good fuck, but she's immature. Chantal is smart and interesting. Well, I'd better get going or I'll be late." I could feel a swish of air as he reached down to kiss me on the forehead. "Goodbye, Elise. It's been fun."

CHAPTER TWENTY-SIX

Chantal combed out her hair in front of the bathroom mirror, applied a coat of luscious lipstick. Mascara, a touch of perfume. Her stomach filled with tiny, fluttering winged creatures. She had not felt this alive, this full of anticipation, in . . . how many years? She couldn't remember now. Her emerald eyes stood out, ringed with black kohl. The camisole clung to her breasts. She wore matching lace panties. She pulled the sheath blouse over the camisole, slid into slinky black leggings. Then she put on a soft sweater, socks, and black flats with treads, for walking on the deck of the yacht. Last, she wound a patterned satin scarf around her neck.

Her phone buzzed in the bedroom. She hurried over, saw Bill's name lighting up the screen. Why did he keep calling? She hit the "Decline" button. He was the one who had left her. He'd made his own bed—he could lie in it now.

There it was, the insistent ring of the doorbell. Chantal checked her reflection one last time—she was irresistible—and smacked her lips. Rushed down the stairs to the foyer. Flung open the door.

There he was, stunning in his sexy black dry suit and wool cap. "Hey," he said, looking around. His gaze caught hers again. She could see the raw hunger in his eyes.

"Right on time," she said, stepping back to let him in. "How did it go?" She looked at him anxiously, studied his face for a sign of trouble, but he grinned, relaxed as usual.

"It went like clockwork," he said. "She found a condom in my pocket. It just made my job easier."

"Good timing then," she said, and let out her breath. This was really happening. He'd really done it. "How was she when you left?"

"Asleep," he said.

"In her bed—she hadn't taken anything else?"

"Her system is clean. Do you think I would be that stupid?"

"No, of course not." Her hands were shaking a little. "It's just . . . strange. Surreal."

"You'll get used to it," he said.

"What about Bella?"

"I dropped her with the babysitter. Don't worry so much. You weren't this anxious when you were making the formula."

"I know—it's just so real."

"You look beautiful."

"So do you," she said.

"You got a waterproof jacket? It could get wet out there."

She laughed. "I do have rain gear, but there's no rain in the forecast."

"Just in case. I like to be prepared."

"So you do."

"A drink before we go?" he said. "Do you have that bottle of rye I gave you?"

"I was hoping you'd say that." She ushered him into the living room, slid over to the liquor cabinet, held up the bottle of Rittenhouse. "I make a mean Manhattan."

Kieran whistled softly. "Can't pass that up. I hope you're having one, too."

"Two Manhattans, coming up."

He walked to the standing glass cabinet, in which she displayed her collection of action figures. "Are these Bill's or yours?"

"They're all mine." She mixed the ingredients of his drink. Bourbon, vermouth, Angostura bitters, etcetera. And a fresh cherry. Then her own.

"Lots of female action figures here," he said. "They look pretty badass."

"They are," she said, bringing him his drink. "Will you be sober enough to drive down to the boat?"

"After one drink? Hell yes," he said, holding up the glass to clink it against hers. "And I can sail the yacht and row the dinghy and stay awake all night with you in our little love nest."

"The cabin is not so little," she said.

They drank without sitting, perhaps both of them jumpy with the truth of what they had done, and with the prickle of anticipation. "This was damned good," he said, holding up his empty glass. "The best Manhattan I've ever had."

"Glad to hear it," she said, relieved. "I was a bartender once."

"Now you're a computer geek," he said. "A hot one."

When she turned around, he was right there in front of her, reaching out to touch her hair. She felt that flutter again, the anticipation of release.

She looked up into his eyes, took his hand in hers, held on. "Wait until we get there. Not here."

"Then let's go. I'm driving."

The interior of the Jaguar smelled clean, not old. She sat in the passenger seat, trying to control her breathing as he drove down to the harbor. "Do you think we should move her?" she asked, testing the water.

"You mean dump her," he said. "No, better she's at home."

"Right," she said, nodding. "You're the doctor."

They were silent for a while.

"Where is this cabin, exactly?" he said.

"You sail us to Orcas Island. I'll get us to the dock."

"How did you find this place?"

"It belongs to a friend," she said. "She stays there like once a year. Wait until you see the inside. It's amazing."

At the harbor, nobody was out on the docks. The boats bobbed on their moorings, reflected in the calm, black waters of the harbor. He helped her onto the yacht, untied the lines, and they were soon on their way, the wind in their hair. She'd been waiting so long.

"We could've just stayed at my house. We would've been alone," she said.

"No, I loved your idea of an adventure," he said. "Elise never liked coming out on the boat. She got seasick."

"Her loss," Chantal said. It didn't take them long to drop anchor in the protected waters off the coast of Orcas. He helped her down the ladder and into the dinghy. He yawned. "Damn. Having the baby around is seriously messing with my sleep patterns." In the bobbing dinghy, he untied the line, picked up the oars. "Where are we headed?"

She pointed up toward the distant lights on a rocky bluff. "There's a dock over there. Does this thing have a motor?"

"It's a tender," he said. "It's not really made for—"

"It's okay. We don't want to make noise anyway," she said. "Until we get to the cabin. Nobody will hear us."

"I like the sound of that." He grinned, yawned again.

After she'd called him a few weeks earlier, it had not taken long for him to respond. Oh, they had flirted for a few years. She had cradled her obsession, nurtured it. But he had never fully come around, not then. If he'd looked in the drawers in her home office, he would've found photographs of himself she'd printed from the internet or taken from a distance with the zoom lens on her camera.

She'd loved Bill, but he'd been the one to buckle beneath the weight of grief. He'd been the one to give up on the marriage, which had filled with blame and accusation, after Jenny's death. Bill had loved Jenny as his own, but he was weak. He'd abdicated his responsibility to the marriage, and Chantal had had no choice but to let him go.

Images of Kieran had rushed in to fill the space. She remembered how he had not turned his back on Jenny, had gone overtime in appointments with her, just to talk, to listen to her concerns. He'd called to check on her, made suggestions for extracurricular activities to keep her occupied, even recommended therapy.

The first date had been three weeks ago, a day after Elise's C-section, when she lay drugged and exhausted in her hospital bed. Chantal had seen Kieran come home to rest for a while and had prepared in her subtle ways. Curled her eyelashes, applied mascara. Chosen a modest long-sleeved knit top that nevertheless revealed her shape, accentuated her curves. Her spandex jogging pants. Practically painted on. She'd taken over homemade muffins, the kind she knew he liked, carrot cake with bits of walnuts. He'd politely offered her coffee—again. And she had offered him an ear and sympathy.

"Elise is so fragile," he said. "She can be exhausting."

"Needy," Chantal said, nodding. "Bill was like that. Wanting me to take care of his emotions."

"The last few weeks have been hard," he said. "She's so damn moody. Up and down. She's mentally unstable."

"Hasn't she always been that way?" Chantal said, reaching out to rub his shoulder. "You're so tense."

"Yeah, work has been rough, too." Dark circles under his eyes.

"You need to relax—did you know I trained to be a massage therapist?"

"Before you became a computer geek? Seriously?" Kieran gave her a wan smile.

"It's been a while, but I think I remember a few things." She stood behind him and began to rub the poor man's stiff shoulders. In another minute he reached up to hold her hand, pulled her down to kiss her. He was good at it, the kissing. Experienced. She was sure he could tie a cherry stem with his tongue.

They'd stolen free moments after that—mainly at her house, not his. Elise had come home a few days after the C-section—hospitals didn't keep people for long—and he'd been preoccupied with caring for her and the baby. But still he slipped away every few days.

"It's such a relief to be with you," he said one morning, stroking Chantal's hair. "Elise is completely paranoid. She's suffering from severe postpartum anxiety."

"What are you going to do about it?" she said, kissing her way from his chest down.

"Do about it?" he said. "What is there to *do* about—" He lost the thread of his thoughts just then.

Afterward, they lamented the way islanders knew everyone's business, the way they gossiped. He admitted to a quick fling with Diane, who had left the island for good. He'd made sure not to be seen with her in public places.

"I wish I could be with you all night," he said, kissing her cheek. "I wish I could be seen with you. I would show you off."

She suggested a new restaurant on Orcas Island—and more. "My friend has a cabin near there, reachable only by boat. There's a protected harbor and a dock."

"My dinghy could make it," he said.

She brought up the idea again the next time he appeared through the woods—oh, to be alone with him!—and he agreed to the getaway.

She told him of her grand plan to sell the house, to move to Mercer Island now that Bill was gone for good and Nick showed no interest in returning to the United States. She showed him the house she coveted.

"Stunning," Kieran said, clicking through the house's spacious rooms on the Realtor's website. He didn't ask how Chantal could afford the place, but she knew he was aching to. If he'd asked, she would've told him about her smart investment decisions, about the stocks in her portfolio that had grown in value exponentially.

"What if I were to go with you, get a job on the island?" he'd said at last, rubbing her arms. "I can't stand the thought of being apart from you."

The plan had taken shape gradually, once it had been made clear—the idea blooming within him as if on its own—that Elise had conspired with Brandon to do him in. And if she'd tried it once, why would she not try again?

Chantal had no answer for that.

He'd finally seen the need for a kind of poetic justice. Giving Elise just the right dosage of the Juliet, doing to her what she and Brandon had tried to do to him. No obvious cause of death would be found—the autopsy results would be inconclusive. He'd wanted to give her an untraceable anesthetic instead, but Chantal had warned him about the paper trail. About how someone might notice at his clinic. She knew what she was doing. "You have to let me mix the powder," she'd said. "Selene taught me how. There are other things in it. Everything works together synergistically."

"All right," he'd said, pulling her down on top of him. "I love that word, *synergistic*."

Now they were on their way to Orcas. He kept rowing the dinghy, but he was slowing down, fumbling with the oars. The little craft was rock solid, though. She knew that a tender like this one, similar to an inflatable Zodiac dinghy, was virtually capsize-proof, unlike a deep-hulled boat. A man could throw his entire weight on the side, and the boat would barely shudder. So she had relaxed, pointing them toward the protected shallow bay on the rugged shoreline and monitoring his increasingly halting progress.

"I might need a nap." He yawned again, his eyelids drooping.

"Want me to row?"

"I'll bring us in . . ." His voice trailed off. His chin bobbed against his chest. He dropped the oars. One nearly fell in the water, but she retrieved it.

"Kieran?" she said.

"Hmmm." He shifted a little, slumped sideways.

She looked toward the island, the shoreline dotted with the lights of distant homes. "Are you feeling all right?"

He mumbled something, groaned.

The waves had begun to rise—the moon was barely a sliver hiding behind the clouds. "Do you know what you drank in the Manhattan?" she asked.

He moaned, mumbled again.

"Yeah, the Juliet," she said. "I messed up the first time. Wrong dose, right?"

"Hmmm," he murmured, and squinted at her. "You . . ."

"I saw Elise out there that night, all those months ago, messing around in the shop, sleepwalking, but then she went back to bed. She always does. She never locks any doors in her sleep. So I went into the shop and I took over for her."

"Hnnnn," he said, his vocabulary in the dumps.

"Brandon didn't know the first thing about mixing a formula. I'd been paying attention, reading the journals, testing things out. He did just what he said he did. He moved you here to the dinghy. Too bad you woke up."

Kieran's lashes fluttered, but he didn't open his eyes.

"You don't remember offering me coffee that morning, do you? Flirting like always."

No response. She hoped he was hearing her, understanding her. She liked to think it was as if he'd fallen down a well, her voice echoing down to him from above.

This was the tricky part—she'd known it would come. She had offered to row the boat, but, of course, he had insisted on doing the hard work. She stood up slowly—still somehow expecting the boat to tip, but the rubber tender was virtually untippable. She leaned over him, grabbed his coat, and heaved him straight forward, past her. The boat shuddered a little as he wiped out face-first on the seat she had just vacated. With all her strength, she shoved him out of the way so she could take up his position at the oars.

She steered the dinghy away from the dock, back out into open water. "I thought it would look like you'd just dropped dead," she said. "I was going to clean up the mess in the shop afterward, but then I heard Elise coming downstairs. I didn't have time. I had to book it out of there."

Kieran's breathing slowed.

"She was so upset about everything. She didn't know what to do. But I did. Or I thought I did. I was so surprised to learn that you'd come back from the dead."

Now he appeared not to breathe at all, and she felt a stab of panic, maybe a touch of guilt? No, not that. "It's funny, but even before I found out about you for sure, every time I saw you, these last few years, I've wanted to kill you. I would feel this need . . . these flutters. It worried me a little, until it didn't anymore. I trusted my instincts and kept an eye on you. Because you're a bad man."

He had killed Jenny, or he might as well have. He'd made her walk into the sea. Chantal knew this.

"Did you really think I would want Elise dead? Or, hell, that I would want to move to Mercer Island? Sorry to tell you—I'm not rich. I never was and probably never will be. I could barely stand having sex with you. I almost threw up. For the record, you slobber." Even now she wanted to scrub the foul memories from her mind. "But I had to do it. I always do what I have to do."

She waited for a reply, but nothing came—only the ripple of waves on the sea, lapping against the side of the dinghy.

"And then I did find out about you for sure," she went on, "when I was helping Elise with her mess. With *you*." She shook her head slowly. When she spoke again, her voice was deeper and broken. "It was a shock to see those pictures on your computer. Of my Jenny. With *you*. Your arm around her, kissing her. My Jenny, naked on your machine? She was just a *girl*. What kind of man are you? Wait, I know. I already knew. I almost smashed your computer."

I hope he's happy now, Jenny had written in her suicide letter. *He.* The boyfriend. She had been seeing someone, secretive as always. Chantal had imagined what the mysterious boyfriend must've said to Jenny to break her heart so completely. *Not interested. It's over. I've got someone new.* Kids could be cruel in high school, she'd thought. But at Kieran's computer, she'd realized the boyfriend had not been a high school student.

"I write back to Jenny," Chantal said to him. "I leave notes on her grave. I like to believe she reads my words, that she knows I love her. I wrote to her that I would never give up on finding the boy—the man—who broke her heart." She stopped for a moment, to let him absorb what she was saying. Then she went on. "I almost told Elise. But I couldn't. The thing is, I suspected you without even knowing I did. There was something about the attention you paid to Jenny. You were so caring. But then you didn't even show up at her memorial service. You sent her favorite flowers, purple hydrangeas in a pot. But you couldn't show your face."

He couldn't hear her—or maybe he could. The hearing was the last thing to go. Or so she'd been told. She gave his shoulder a little shake where he lay, his face mashed against the rubber side of the dinghy.

It was difficult for Chantal to maneuver him, to push him. After much frustration, much heaving, she finally managed to angle his head and shoulders over the side, then work him forward until his center of gravity began to shift. She let him teeter there for a moment. "This is for Elise and Bella," Chantal said. "But most of all, this is for Jenny, for my sweet baby girl." Then she stood, gripped his feet, and heaved them skyward. The boat tipped only a little, its stability working to her advantage as he slipped almost soundlessly into the sea, barely a splash, his body sinking swiftly out of sight.

CHAPTER TWENTY-SEVEN

Chantal floored the Kia on the way home. *Please, please,* she thought in a continuous mantra. *Let me get there in time.*

When she had returned the yacht to the harbor, it had been well past midnight. She had pretended to have no knowledge of sailing as Kieran had navigated out of the harbor. She had let him work on his own. He'd been susceptible to flattery.

After she had dumped him and rowed back to the yacht, she had set the dinghy free, halfway between Orcas and Chinook Islands. Then she had moored the *Knot on Call* to its usual slip in the harbor. Not a soul had been around, and anyway, so what if anyone had seen her? Just a woman walking along the dock.

She had pulled up her hood, jogged down the road to her Kia, which she had parked on the shoulder the day before. She had ridden her bicycle all the way home, a workout, but she was used to it.

Her hands were numb now, and she shivered as she pressed her foot to the accelerator, rubbed the fingers of her left hand, three of which Mike had broken all those years ago. They had healed wrong, still ached sometimes when the weather was cold and damp. As she raced past the graveyard, where he and Jenny were buried, Chantal thought about every time she had tried to leave and he had tracked her down, had hauled her home, had torn out a handful of her hair once. Her scalp tingled at the memory. She'd believed Mike could walk through walls, that he would find her and kill her no matter where she was. Selene had told her to be careful with the Slumber powder—*only a couple of teaspoons to make him sleep long enough,* Selene had said. *To help you get away.* But Chantal had dumped the whole bag of powder into his energy drink. That had been the first time, when she had still been Chantal Farrell, C. Farrell in Selene's journal, married to Mike Farrell. The second time had been the morning she'd dosed Kieran's coffee, without Selene around to check the mixture. Chantal had done her best.

It took forever to reach Lost Bluff Lane. She parked next to Elise's Honda, tore through the garden to the back door. Pulled Kieran's keys from her pocket—he hadn't even noticed that she'd stolen them from his pocket—and let herself in. The house was dark, save for the hood light over the stove.

She turned on the lights as she moved from room to room. She found Elise lying in the bed in the library. Her eyes were half-open, and she was pale and unmoving.

"You didn't get the full dose," Chantal said. "Not even close. Wake up!"

No response from Elise, and she did not appear to be breathing.

What if Chantal had made a mistake again? *No, I didn't. This time I knew what to do.* She ran into the kitchen, ejected some ice cubes from the freezer, filled a glass with water and ice, grabbed a dish towel, ran back to the library. She dipped the cold dish towel into the water, dabbed at Elise's forehead, her cheeks.

"Elise! Wake up." Chantal shook her, rubbed the palms of her hands. Elise's fingers were limp. "I got back as fast as I could," Chantal went on. "I thought you would be awake by now. I made a mild blend. He didn't have enough to kill you, even if he gave you the whole bag. I'm so sorry—I needed to know for sure that he was a killer. I was hoping he wouldn't go through with it . . . but he did. I almost lost it. But I kept my cool. You have to wake up. We'll go to the babysitter and pick up Bella, and it'll be like none of this ever happened. Like *he* never happened. You'll both be safe. Okay? He's not coming back this time, not ever again. Please, Elise."

Chantal rested her head on Elise's unmoving arm. How could this be happening? She should never have allowed Kieran to try this. But then Elise would have always been running away, and Chantal would never be at peace. Who knew what he would have done? Elise had returned to trusting him, thinking Brandon had tried to kill him. "It was never Brandon," Chantal said, pushing Elise's hair away from her forehead. "It was always me."

Did a finger twitch? Was that a touch of pink in her cheeks? Yes, and a sharp intake of breath, an exhale. Then a gasp. Elise stirred, gasped again. Her lashes fluttered. She opened her eyes, looked around. Her chest rose and fell. The color returned to her skin. A growing panic crossed her face as she bolted upright. "Where am I? What are you doing here?"

Chantal wiped the tears from her cheeks and laughed. "Welcome back to the world, my friend."

EPILOGUE

"Mama, Mama!" Bella runs toward the shop in the sunlight. I'm standing behind the counter, ringing up a tonic for Deputy John Russell. We both turn toward her as she bursts inside. Her hair shines blonde—someone must've had hair that color back a few generations. Certainly not me and neither of my parents. And not Kieran. His hair was darker. She's got my brown eyes, not Kieran's blue ones. But sometimes, when she frowns or turns a certain way, I can see a flash of him in her, like a phantom, and then it's gone.

"What is it?" I say, bending down to hug her.

"Hey, Bella," John says, smiling.

"Hey, Uncle John," she says. "I need to talk to my mom."

"Go right ahead," he says, "but you owe me a bike ride in the park. I'll push you with the training wheels?"

"Tomorrow," she says, her voice sober. "This is really important."

"Okay, then. Tomorrow it is. Promise?"

"It's a date," she says, nodding vigorously.

He tousles her hair, grabs his bag of tonics and tinctures, and heads for the door. When he gets there, he turns to wink at me, and I smile. He has been a good friend all these years. Dependable, loyal, a fun uncle for Bella. Almost like a father.

After he leaves, I crouch down to look into her eyes. She's so worried; I can tell. She's clutching something in the palm of her hand, something hidden.

Out of the corner of my eye, I can see Chantal through the sashed windows, standing in the garden to adjust her sun hat. She's helping me tend to the vegetables. Soon we'll harvest beans, broccoli, and cherry tomatoes to donate to the food bank. She glances our way and waves at us with one gloved hand. I wave back. She's probably thinking what I'm thinking, hoping four-year-old Bella has not found another poor baby bird that somehow fell from the nest. Or a squished caterpillar for which we'll have to perform a funeral.

Bella's compassion expands to fill the world. Where there is barren soil, she plants a seed. Where there is destruction, she creates hope. Where darkness has spread, she breathes light.

"A fairy lost a wing," Bella says soberly, sitting up on a stool at the counter. She's in a sunflower dress—she herself in constant bloom now, although she was not an easy baby. I didn't sleep much after Kieran disappeared. Sometimes I wake from a nightmare in which he has returned from the dead, covered in seaweed, to kill Bella and me. I can still imagine he's out there alive somewhere, although I know he is not. His dinghy was found floating out beyond the island, but his body was never recovered.

Chantal told me everything that night, after we brought Bella home from the babysitter's house. About how she saw photographs of Kieran and Jenny on his computer when we broke into his farmhouse. About how she had thought about killing him and how to do it. She had failed the first time—Brandon had been deranged but not a murderer—and she was going to try again, but then she had realized how much Bella and I needed him. She had been conflicted.

But when she'd felt I no longer needed Kieran to help care for Bella, and when she thought he might kill me at any time, Chantal had seduced him, and he had readily slept with her. She had pretended to support him, to covet material things as he did. He had admitted to wanting me dead, but he'd been waiting for Bella to be born. He couldn't kill his own child.

I don't remember eating the bread or drinking the tea, which Chantal said I'd done. I don't remember what Kieran might have said to me before he walked out. But I know he gave me the Juliet powder, which Chantal had mixed up and had assured him was lethal. The last thing I recall, even today, is finding the telephone number and condom in his clothes. I don't even remember him coming back into the house. In my mind, he's forever out in the driveway, returning calls.

My husband tried to kill me.

My husband tried to kill me.

When I tell myself these words, they don't seem real. I feared Bella would become like him, but I needn't have worried. Her restlessness, her crying and sensitivity, reflected her early empathy, her awareness of the world as both a beautiful and terrible place, full of happiness but also heartache and suffering. And she felt—she feels—all of it. I don't know how—she is just wired that way. As if the universe needed to tip the balance, to right itself.

She lifts her closed fist to me, her eyes bright with tears. "We have to find the fairy. It lost a wing."

"Show me," I said, dreading what she carries in her hand.

Chantal smiles in our direction, her shiny hair catching the sunlight. She nods slightly as Bella opens her hand to reveal a delicate, translucent pink rose petal in the shape of a heart, and I feel a twinge of memory, a recollection of a heart-shaped anniversary card from years ago, better left in the past. "See?" she says. "It was on the ground. All by itself. She can't fly. The fairy can't fly without her wing."

"Yes, she can," I say. "Not many people know this, but fairies have special powers."

Bella's large brown eyes grow even wider. "They do?" she whispers.

"Yes," I say, hugging her. "When fairies lose their wings, they're shedding them, leaving them behind. The fairy left her wing on purpose for you to find. When the wings fall off, they always grow back. Soon she'll be flying again."

"Oh, goodie!" Bella laughs, buoyant once more.

She is everything now—morning, night, darkness, and light. I close her little hand around the petal, relieved to know that she has not picked a flower from the Juliet plant, which has not reappeared since her birth. But we stay vigilant, Chantal and I, for any sign, for we know what the plant can do.

ACKNOWLEDGMENTS

As always, I'm deeply grateful to my brilliant editor at Lake Union Publishing, Danielle Marshall; fabulous developmental editor, David Downing; literary agent extraordinaire, Paige Wheeler; and the entire production and author relations teams at Amazon Publishing, including but not limited to Nicole Pomeroy, Gabriella T. Dumpit, Kristin King, James Gallagher, Kellie Osborne, and Elise Taubenheim. I depend on valuable input from my incomparable writing peeps. Sandy Dengler, Anne Clermont, and Leigh Hearon came through with excellent comments at the eleventh hour. I'm also grateful to Susan Wiggs, Sheila Roberts, Kate Breslin, Elsa Watson, Randall Platt, Patricia M. Stricklin, Lois Dyer, and Dianne Gardner. I received valuable information and feedback from Detective Glenn Kerns, Ret., Seattle PD; Stephen Messer; Dr. Don Williamson; Rich Penner; Marilyn Lundberg, LCSW; Annis Pepion Scott and Professor Donald Edward Scott; Paula Siddons; and my amazing early readers—you are the best. Thank you to Karyn Schwartz, proprietor of the wonderful SugarPill Apothecary in Seattle, for a fascinating interview. I'm grateful to all the supportive bloggers and reviewers who've shouted out about my books, and the readers who've contacted me to say they love my novels.

AUTHOR'S NOTE

Thank you so much for reading *The Poison Garden*! I hope you enjoyed the journey. I love setting novels in the mysterious, wild environs of Washington State, where I currently live in a cottage in the woods. Chinook Island, featured in this book, is not a real place but a fictional amalgam of Pacific Northwest islands I've visited: Whidbey Island, Orcas Island, San Juan Island, and Vashon Island.

Also, while the physician in the story may have shady leanings, he does not represent most doctors. I appreciate ethical medical practitioners everywhere, especially my own family physician, an exceptionally gifted and compassionate man, who even called in a prescription for cough syrup in the middle of the night on Christmas Eve for me one year when I had the flu. All characters in this book, and the deadly Juliet plant, are figments of my fiendish imagination.

ABOUT THE AUTHOR

Photo © 2015 Carol Ann Morris

Born in India and raised in North America, A. J. Banner received degrees from the University of California, Berkeley. Her previous novels of psychological suspense include the bestsellers *The Good Neighbor* and *After Nightfall*. She lives in the Pacific Northwest with her husband and six rescued cats. For more information, visit www.ajbanner.com.